THE WAKE AND THE MANUSCRIPT

THE WAKE

and the manuscript

ANSGAR ALLEN

The Wake and the Manuscript

Copyright © 2022 by Ansgar Allen

ISBN: 978-0-99-915359-8

Library of Congress Number: 2022940888

First Anti-Oedipal Paperback Edition, December 2022

www.rawdogscreaming.com

Cover Artwork by Jacobello Alberegno

"Polyptych of the Apocalypse" (14th Century)

Revelation 20:11-12

Cover and Interior Design by D. Harlan Wilson

www.dharlanwilson.com

Anti-Oedipus Press

Grand Rapids, MI

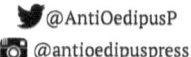@AntiOedipusP

@antioedipuspress

www.anti-oedipuspress.com

To my father.

he invitation was a pretext. I was the family friend, the oldest friend this family could remember, but I was invited as a writer and a thinker, I came to think. My role was not to mourn with the rest of them. This soon became apparent. I was not supposed to mourn at all.

My daughter walked me to the gate, I told her to leave me there. We had been arguing, first in the car, and then beside it. She stood holding the keys and looked at me with that look she had. When she was a little girl she would stand like that. I did not remind her of it as I thought, looking at her, how much you remind me of the way you stood when you were little. Only now she could justify her rage to me and would do so when it subsided. She would justify it in terms I would understand and could not escape. When her rage subsided, she would do this to me, even days later she would return to this event and go over it in her mind and then go over it with me. And if she didn't bring it up again, I would still look at her and know what she was doing. This is how children develop into adults, I thought. Children learn to carry their rage with them and turn it over in their minds and so become adults. They give sense to their rage and make it far worse for that reason, turning it into the articulated rage of adulthood which persists with the unarticulated rage of infancy. When her anger subsided, she would begin the work of justifying it to herself so that I could not escape this moment like every other example of my apparent *bad nature* that she still turns over in her mind. We have always caused each other pain and she carries that tension with her. This occasion was like any other. It set her off. For the entire journey I sat and read Thomas Bernhard's *Extinction*. It was not the first time. I know the book well. I am an avid reader of Bernhard's work. I have been reading Bernhard ever since he was first translated. I consider myself to be one of the first readers of Bernhard in translation as well as a prolific re-reader. My daughter knows well that I re-read Bernhard's books at regular intervals. If I feel that a little Bernhard might be necessary, I go to the shelf and read again another of my Bernhard books that she has seen me read, or hold, several times before. I say to her, as I have often said, it is time for a little Bernhard, and I take a Bernhard book down from the shelf, any book is as good as any other, and sit with it until she leaves. My daughter is familiar with situations like this. What really finished her off was not my reading or my silence, or my refusal to answer her questions about what we should do with mother—by which she meant her mother's ashes. She tolerated the fact that when she repeatedly asked me, as she drove, what we should do about mother, I repeatedly ignored her. It was not the fact that I ignored her, or my reading habit that did her in, as it had not done her in before, and she was entirely used to it. For the whole journey I refused to answer that question about mother and set about reading *Extinction*, and this she tolerated as she had tolerated situations like that often enough. She asked me her question about mother, about what we should do with mother and so on, and I did raise my head at the question, but then looked back to *Extinction* and continued reading. But when I got out of the car, I made as if to take *Extinction* with me. That is to say, as I opened the passenger door it became apparent to her that I was taking *Extinction* with me to the wake. She knew, as she saw me move, that I was about to take that book to the wake and would sit with it alongside the mourners who would have nothing with them but their grief, or their show of grief, and would look up at me sitting with a book called *Extinction* on my lap. I would sit before them, waiting for the right moment to continue reading, and that is why I had to take *Extinction* with me. It enraged her to see me do that, even though she had coped very well with my refusal to answer her question about mother, even though it would actually be a very good idea to have *Extinction* under my arm at the wake, I thought, just in case I needed it, so that if there was a moment when reading would help, or if there was a lull, I would have something to look at. But when she saw me begin to carry *Extinction* out of the car, and tuck it under my arm, she went very nearly mad. It surprised me that she went so very nearly mad at that, having not complained about my reading of *Extinction* in the car, or my refusal to answer her questions about what to do with mother. She sat for a while, enraged, and then got out of the car and stood before me holding the keys in her fist, entirely consumed by her anger, by the rage which now took hold of her and that she would later go on to justify. I thought she looked a little hunched. Looking at her, I thought to myself, you do look a little hunched. As she stood like that, she looked at me just as she did when she was a little girl, an unflinching, determined look, and absolutely refused to leave unless it was with Bernhard's *Extinction*. She refused point blank, and so to save myself embarrassment, I gave it to her immediately regretting my decision. I handed *Extinction* over and felt, as soon as I did, that it was the wrong thing to do and that I would suffer because of it. I walked down the path to the front door of the house and thought that it was the wrong decision, it was a mistake to hand over *Extinction*, but now there was no getting it back. She was holding it, and would go with it, and leave me here at the wake without it to look at should I need it. But there was no way I would ask her for it back, or that she would give it to me if I asked. I approached the house knowing that, complaining to myself at my decision to hand it to her. The son of the deceased was at the door. I stood there with my back to my daughter at the gate, or in the car, and extended a hand to the son with my condolences, thinking as I did so about Bernhard's *Extinction* and my decision to hand it over. The son gave me a stack of paper to hold. It was a manuscript, or hardly that. A mere typewritten stack, I told myself as I continued to think about my mistake, about how I had given in too easily to my daughter and her rage. This son has just passed me a mere typewritten stack, I thought, wondering still about Bernhard's *Extinction*. No sooner have I arrived at the house and the son takes the first opportunity to give me a stack of paper, an entirely redundant stack of paper which I knew instantly to be his father's work. This typewritten manuscript, as I knew well, was the output of an exhausted mind, a failed mind. It was a product of his father's failure. There was nothing in it worth paying any kind of attention to, or at least, there was no way of reading this manuscript without thinking, *this manuscript is the expression of a failed mind, a mind which exhausted itself needlessly*. And then, to make things worse, the son said to me, *You must make something of these*, referring to the papers left by his father. I hardly responded to his request to *make something of these* due to my surprise at the bundle and the words that came with it. I did also still have the memory, the muscle sensation, of Bernhard's *Extinction* in my hand, and it pained me to hold this manuscript instead. But more than that, I was preoccupied by the more serious thought, the one on my mind for the entire drive over, that I was in some way responsible for his father's death. As my daughter went on about her mother, I was thinking of his father. When he passed me the manuscript and asked me to *make something of these*, I was still thinking about his father's death, and whether or not I was responsible for it. His father would have died anyway, I decided, deciding that again as I had decided it before, although I could not quite rid myself of the memory, the notion, that I had a hand in it. I stood there at the front door and received the papers, and thought to myself, *I very probably had a hand in your father's death*. As the son welcomed me in, I repeated to myself the additional and crucial fact, *but I did not kill him*. When the son closed the door and laid a gentle hand on my shoulder, I decided that having a hand in his father's death was not the same as killing him. I did not kill his father. I did not kill your father, I thought, as the son ushered me down the hallway, a hallway I knew well, saying as he ushered me on how glad he was that I had accepted the manuscript and how pleased he was that I would *make something of it*, indicating the papers, and as he did so I nodded, and continued to think about his father's death, and the circumstances of it, and what had led him to it, and so on, and then, naturally, what my involvement might have been, etcetera, how culpable I was, and so on down the hallway. I proceeded to the dining room in which the deceased had been put on the table, carefully laid out and dressed. At the head end I paid my respects, or said something, I think I said something as I looked down at his face. His lips were thin, but his lips were always thin. Since he was little, they looked like that. When we were children I was already struck by the thinness of his lips. I suspect I teased him for it. Now the same lips were pressed and dry. As I looked, I fancied, just for a moment, that I saw the last crease of a smile. The man seemed to smile or be caught in the last moments of a grin, at me, or the ceiling, but then appeared not to smile at me, or the ceiling, his mouth lifeless with nothing at the edges of it. The papers I held were embarrassing to me. The son had no idea. The son had given me the entire stack, his father's legacy in print, but had absolutely no idea, none at all, about their contents. He would not know but could have known, indeed should have known, had he attended to his studies and studied his father in turn. He would have seen that these papers testified to his father's persistent failure to think or write in a way that others, such as myself, would find themselves able to rate as worthwhile output and place alongside our own writing as if he were our peer and not a nuisance at the faculty to which I belonged. His father's tendency in writing and thought, beyond a certain intellectual laziness, was to over-reach himself and say more than he ought. His father, I thought, looking over at the son, always said more than others wanted to hear. He would visit us at the university on the basis of some privilege he received, years ago, an honorary lectureship. Even then it must have been an act of generosity approaching pity to give him that lecture-ship, which was not a proper lectureship, merely an honorary one. It came with no responsibilities, and no salary, just the privilege such as it was, which he took as permission to come visit as if he were a fellow member of staff and our intellectual peer. These papers I now held at the head end of the deceased were very much like the stack I recalled him with as he wandered along our corridors, only it was much larger now, thicker, more disorderly. He would walk with his papers and we would retreat. We would see him approaching and find some excuse to turn about. A typewritten wad of failed thoughts and false ideas, I thought. The son clearly believed they were worth something even though they reeked of failure, his father's smell. Certain men reach a certain age and begin to reek in that way. His father was like that. I could smell it on him. It was obvious with men like this, with men like his father, that this was it, there was no backing out of their failure.

And still his father carried on, writing as he did, and burdened the rest of us with writing that embarrassed us. It was obvious just by looking at it, and by looking at him holding it, that it would be a painful read. I had always avoided his writing, knowing what pain it would cause, and so the contents of this particular manuscript were largely a mystery to me. The edges of it testified by their unevenness, and their lack of binding, or even just proper organisation, that his failure in life to assemble his thinking was finally executed in death. This was the extent of his accomplishment. These pages. I held them at the head end, at the head of the table, as if it were my job to put them to the earth with the rest of him. As I held them, I saw him already in his hole, my role to toss these pages, the entire wad, into the grave. Chief among mourners, first to feel relief. The first clod of mud, and then the papers. The dead man, and then the dead prospect of his work. The mud, the work, and his failure to live. I would have laughed at the man and the wad he left me with, at the absurd mission I had been given, at the stupidity of his son, but for the company. I would have laughed at him *as his friend* of course, as his life-long friend, or at least as his life-long acquaintance, a knowing laugh of our own drawn-out association, the laugh of someone who has been more or less forced to associate with someone else since childhood and knows too well what he is dealing with. Even though we did have our differences, which were chiefly intellectual in kind, he regarded me, as he would often say, as his life-long friend, whereas I regarded him as a life-long acquaintance. We will be friends until you die, he would say. Until you die there will be no separating us, he said, and I would stand listening to him say it and fear that he was probably right. I stood at the head end of the dining table—extended at the middle to its full length, to the necessary length—and saw him already in his hole. I saw him lying down there waiting to receive his manuscript, and I saw myself ready to drop it on him. It was probably my guilt at thinking that, a grotesque and unseemly thought presenting itself at precisely this moment, at the worst possible moment, which led me to volunteer, in that state of guilt, to sit up with the son all night. It was expected that the deceased would be sat with until morning at which point the vigil would be over. This was his dying wish. There was no tradition of it in his family, and the idea of a wake was alien to this particular version of the church, the church he was now a member of. But it was his wish, and he was a peculiar man, a burdensome man, as I have often thought. This was his final imposition. He imposed his final wish upon us by demanding a wake. The son obeyed. I volunteered. The dead man had his way. The son seemed to appreciate my offer, or he accepted at least, after which he took the more comfortable seat. Neither of us knew what to do at a wake, not really. We had no clear idea what was expected of us, I thought, as he took the more comfortable seat. Sitting itself was clearly on the list of expectations, and so he took that seat. I could not fail to notice the decisive manner in which he went over to that seat on which he fell into a kind of sleep, leaving me with the more upright chair and the stack of papers. You must make something of these, his son had said, after which I had thought something nasty about the papers, I had to admit, and the man, his father, about putting the stack to the earth with the rest of him, which was hardly appropriate but entirely deserved. It was inevitable that I would end up looking at these papers, despite my understandable reluctance, I thought. The décor, the carpet and so on could only hold my interest for so long. The carpet was actually tasteless, and I refused to look at the dead father for obvious reasons. There is no way to look at the dead. Those who look at the dead never actually look at the dead, I have often thought, they only appear to look because their minds are clouded. Most would prefer not to, or only look when looking is expected, but otherwise look away, their minds then clouded by the idea of not looking. I did not look, and my mind was clouded for that reason. My chair faced him directly, the dead father, but also the son, or the idiot son as I now called him, which was not fair, I knew, it was completely uncalled for to refer to him, as I did, as the idiot son, even though it had been decidedly unfair of him to burden me with his father's manuscript. My chair was set to the left as the father lay and was arranged so that I sat in line with his ear. The son was opposite on the other side of the room facing the other side of his father, the right-hand side as his father lay. It seemed impolite to rearrange the furniture, or, if not impolite, simply impossible, as if unthinkable that I should stand up, turn my chair by a sufficient angle so that I did not have to stare at the deceased, or more precisely, so that I did not have to constantly avoid staring at the man, the side of the face, the ear, whose vigil we were holding. The pile of papers offered a kind of refuge, although in any other situation they would repel me, not even bore me, but actively repel me, more than they did, just as his father's thought had repelled me, or his attempts to think, in life. As I glanced down and began to regard the pile with studied disinterest, I noticed a page that appeared to have some status, since it was near the top, was typed out more carefully, and began with a degree of pomp that the author, now dead, would have thought fitting for a book-opening remark. This page was probably in its intended place, in the wad, unlike other parts of the stack that appeared to have been dropped and gathered without any understanding of their contents. Some pages were even facing the wrong way. That, undoubtedly, was the son's contribution. This was the work of the idiot son, I thought, although it was not fair of me to call him that, I knew, and I really should relent before the expression takes hold in my mind. The son, I told myself, the son, not the idiot son, the son, had no appreciation of his father's work. Having dropped it, he would have merely bunched it back together after it had fallen, not knowing how one page linked to the next page due to his inability to understand the nature of his father's work and thereby perceive both its logic—which gave it a certain internal order—and its illogic, or falseness, which was the reason for its neglect by all but the author, now dead. Above this particular page, the one with some status, was a series of other pages, preliminary ones, largely blank but with titles, more often than not crossed out and replaced with other titles, or commentaries on titles, as if no title would satisfy the job of summing up the work. This was typical, I thought. The page I took from below these preliminaries was, moreover, directly underneath a severely dog-eared piece of paper that turned out to be a contents page of sorts, or an attempt at writing a page of contents that had been edited and overwritten to near oblivion. The basic order of chapters remained the same—and there were too many of them—but all the titles, it seemed, had to be scrubbed out and adjusted. It was as if he expended all his doubt in the title pages and the contents page, leaving none, no doubt at all, for the rest of the manuscript which had been bashed out on his typewriter with ruthless determination. The page which had the feeling of the first page of the first chapter began with a quote from Aristotle that immediately put me off going any further. It was disgusting and pretentious. This was both a disgusting and a pretentious way to begin a book, I thought. But the immediate surroundings were off-putting too. The surroundings were actually hostile, I thought. These surroundings were pressing on me and prompting me to wonder again if I had a hand in his death, whether I might even be considered the cause of it. As I sat there, and wondered if I had or not, I then consoled myself with the thought that causing someone's death is not the same as killing them. Even if I caused his death, or had some hand in it, I did not kill him, I decided, but the thought of killing him still pressed on me. I did not kill him, I told myself again, but telling myself that still made me feel sick. Even if causing, or having some hand in his death, was not the same as actually killing him, the thought of it still tugged at me. Actually, no, he effectively killed himself. I did not kill him, he killed himself, I told myself, because in effect that's what he did. By effectively killing himself he even made it look as if I caused it, as if I had some hand in it, whereas he did it all, it was done as he decided, as he determined. I had to admit that if he did kill himself, he didn't do it in the conventional sense. This is what made it so difficult to determine. He didn't actually kill himself, not in the typical sense, but he did at least cause his death, or put himself in such a position that I might have well caused it, although I didn't. The thought of it all still oppressed me. I simply could not exculpate myself under these conditions. These surroundings are hostile, I reflected, and it is a mistake to be here, I thought. Even without my suspicion regarding the cause of his death and my own culpability in it, the surroundings themselves were against me, they pressed on me, the corpse on the table, the son across the room. There was enough reason here to return to the page in question even if it was pretentious and disgusting. To begin his manuscript with Aristotle like that is utterly pretentious, I repeated to myself. And the content is disgusting. I looked up. But the corpse. So I looked back down. There is no way of looking at the dead. The chair on which I sat was to all effects unmovable as if I suffered some kind of paralysis in relation to its position, a kind of social paralysis facing the corpse, or a paralysis in manners. Good manners are basically instruments of paralysis, I thought. We learn good manners and paralyse ourselves with them. It was a shame that I had such good manners, I decided. If I didn't have such good manners, I would move my chair. But I continued instead with the quote from Aristotle which read, *The child gives a cry and puts its hands up to its mouth as soon as it issues forth.* I looked up for a moment at the death scene, and then back down. *Moreover, the child voids excrement sometimes at once, sometimes a little later, but in all cases during the first day; and this excrement is unduly copious in comparison with the size of the child; it is what the midwives call the meconium or 'poppy-juice.'* This stirred a memory. I had come across meconium and how it resembles poppy juice somewhere before. *In colour it resembles blood, extremely dark and pitch-like, but later on it becomes milky, for the child takes at once to the breast. Before birth the child makes no sound, even though in difficult labour it put forth its head while the rest of the body remains within.* And that was it, the quote was over. He had bashed it out on his typewriter with portentous seriousness amusing himself no doubt with Aristotle's birth scene, with the child that *gives a cry and puts its hands up to its mouth as soon as it issues forth.* He typed out, *the child voids excrement,* and probably thought himself very clever as he noted, Aristotle notes, that *this excrement is unduly copious,* as well as *dark and pitch-like,* and that it resembles what *the midwives call the meconium or 'poppy-juice.'* Very clever indeed. *This excrement is unduly copious,* he bashed out on his machine. *This excrement is unduly copious,* he wrote. *This excrement is unduly copious,* he typed, sitting there as he did so, thinking as he typed, how well-chosen this birth scene, this Aristotelian birth scene, and how perfectly it set up his argument. I looked up again at the death scene and thought for a moment about the fact of his birth, about the fact that even he, now dead, was once born. I could scarcely imagine that the man, the dead man, had once been small and covered with fluid, perhaps even with excrement. In abstract I could conceive of his birth, it was logical that he had been born, but I could not imagine it. His birth was inconceivable, especially so in the presence of his corpse. This quote from Aristotle, which seemed an odd place to begin, was followed by a paragraph that offered something by way of explanation, even though it actually did nothing of the sort. Aristotle places the root of Western education in the soil of its children, he wrote just after the quote. The root of Western education is quite clearly placed, he went on somewhat repeating himself, in the soil of its children. By which he meant in the excrement of its children, thinking himself very clever in thinking that. The root of Western education is to be found in the excrement of its children, was what he meant. Education from excrement—that was the gist of his argument. In this birth scene, Aristotle, he continued, accompanies the traditional oral examination—a respected feature of Western education—with an anal one, and records the first act of the child, to cry out, and then excrete. *The child gives a cry and puts its hands up*, and then excretes, I read. The shit, he wrote, always comes after birth, he went on, but sometimes also before, as with the distressed child that expels faecal matter on its way into the world and so arrives with the meconium it passed within. When the unborn child is distressed, he continued, again repeating himself somewhat, it excretes its way into the world. Faecal matter arrives first. Then the child. If the meconium is thick, the child is distressed. If the meconium is the consistency of pea soup, the birth will be difficult, he wrote. *The child voids excrement*, he repeated, thinking himself clever, and if this excrement is unduly thick, he went on, there will be complications. I paused. I knew well enough that meconium arrives like that, as a signal of distress. I have heard women talk of it. Meconium precedes the child and signals a difficult labour, complications perhaps, and sends midwives into a different mode of action. You arrive at hospital, so I am told, and need only mention the word meconium, or describe how it looks, and the receiving midwife ushers you from the birthing pool to the emergency suite where they strap on devices to measure the heartbeat, and so on. We did not have birthing pools when my children were born, it was done in a room. Childbirth took place in a room, and the room was a simple one. There was a special bed for it, if that, and that was about it. All the paraphernalia of birth did not yet exist, only the spectacle of birth, and that was enough, if not already too much. The whole spectacle of birth has always struck me as deeply unpleasant. I have always failed to understand why anyone could describe it as a moment of *wonder*, when the whole thing is merely unpleasant, not to mention painful, and dangerous, even deadly. I avoided the birth of my own children. Actually, I did not avoid each birth, there was no expectation back then that the father should be present. It was not a fatherly thing to attend the birth of one's children when my children were born. It was not expected for the man to stand, or pace about, or hold the hand of the mother, his beloved, or say things that might help, although nothing helps, so I understand, when it comes to childbirth. Fathers did not stand, and sweat, and worry, and recoil, and say soothing things which are always the wrong things, and retch, and tear up, and get carried away with themselves, before finally seeing how puny, how pointless, how utterly ineffectual men are before the spectacle of a woman in labour. Men had no idea, back then, how puny they were, so I understand. The puniness of men was not well understood. They were not confronted with the miserable plight of a woman in labour and so were not confronted with their own insignificance in that moment where the man has no role to play, not really, only given roles such as cutting the umbilical—that utterly disgusting, prototypically *manly* custom—or submitting to a woman's grip that drains all blood from the gripped hand, pain over which the man cannot complain since his pain is nothing alongside the pain of giving birth, so they say. Men did not come to realise that even their suffering means nothing before the spectacle of birth, and that all they are left with are given roles, and given duties, not that men today realise this all that much, I suspect, and not that this realisation changes anything about their outlook, because the moment of birth is swiftly forgotten, as every birth needs to be forgotten in its details, because each birth is an unpleasant event much better not thought about or recalled by all who might recollect it. I did not attend the birth of my children and would not attend if I had the opportunity, and so have no real knowledge myself of birth, as I am sure he never attended the birth of his children either. It was not expected of him. He was nothing but a birth listener at best, not even a birth spectator, a birth listener waiting for the steps of the nurse, or the midwife, or the doctor, who would deliver the news from a birthing room which, as far as he was concerned, was a distant place, or was sufficiently distant for him not to see his own puniness before it. When his son arrived, he was not there. Perhaps he was nearby, but he was not really there. And here he was writing about meconium, turning meconium into the basis of his argument, instrumentalising meconium and the suffering of all women on the opening pages of his manuscript, which was really just a wad of paper. It was unpleasant to me, there are limits to my tolerance, but still not half as unpleasant as having to sit here before the man and look at the ear. The ordure of the child is the first to be reformed, Aristotle notes, he wrote. Meconium shit turns into regular shit, or less irregular shit. The child draws from the breast and begins to shit differently, he added, building up to the claim, his most fundamental claim, namely, that the education of the child is inaugurated in this manner of its adjusted shitting. The education of the child, he had written, begins with the first adjustment in the manner of its shitting, or something like that, where all that follows is recorded, he went on, and becomes the story of its development. The reformation of shit, the production of new-born shit, milk-reformed shit replacing meconium shit, announces the beginning of education, he wrote. Education, he went on, begins at birth as the child submits to inspection from the rear end to the mouth, and as it submits to adjustment, again from rear to mouth. The child's first products—shit and inchoate sound—define the object to be educated as they are turned over and discussed. Examined excreta and examined sound declare the mission of education, he wrote, which is to reform and correct. One of the first tasks is to inspect and then regulate toilet habits and teach disgust before excrement. It is a much-neglected fact that children have no disgust before what they excrete, he wrote. If only we thought a little more about the teaching of that disgust we would understand a lot more about the origins of education, he went on. Education originates in the examination of excreta, he wrote. Look at the shit a child produces, listen to the sound it makes, and see just how much work must be done to *bring it up*. Sound must be rendered intelligible, shit will be policed, and so on, he wrote. That is where education began, etcetera. And still begins, and so on again. In ancient Greek shit, etcetera. I looked up at the man who had once written these words. The arms. The fingers. Reading these words and thinking these thoughts is what I have been reduced to, I reflected, sitting at the wake. I was invited to this wake not to mourn, but to make something of this wad of paper. I was brought here not as the family friend, as the oldest friend this family could recall, but as a writer and a thinker. I was invited on a pretext so that I might begin work on the stack of paper, on his so-called *Nachlass*, and here I was already at it, reading his work that very night. Reading these pages is my penance for a moment of guilt I did not deserve since the thoughts I had at the head end of the body were entirely justifiable thoughts. They merely occurred when other thoughts should have been happening, according to convention, although who knows exactly what happens inside the heads of those who attend the dead, many of whom probably spend most of the time, despite their best intentions, with their minds elsewhere, what to have for dinner, for instance, or the thing which is happening next week, and so on. I have been to many funerals and found my mind wandering. It is entirely understandable that my mind would wander at a funeral. Those who attend funerals should forgive themselves for thinking about other things. It is almost impossible to focus on the presence of death, I knew. And so, although I avoided him when he lived, avoiding the thought of death had returned me to his writing. I now found myself compelled to read his manuscript, first obliged to hold his papers, and then forced by my good manners and a moment of guilt to attend his vigil. These are the unfortunate events that brought me to sit here with no other distraction from the sight of his body but the writings he left, and that no publisher would touch, nor colleague of mine for that matter, because it was professionally embarrassing to touch anything he had written. To claim that the Western educational experience, which must include everything from poetry and art to philosophy, religion, and science, originates in the inspection and ordering of shit, was just exactly the kind of rubbish he would produce. It was obvious to me that what he envisaged here was to return to and foul upon one of the so-called originating thinkers of Western thought by claiming, quite cleverly he must have believed, that Aristotle himself provides the clue to the origins of Western education in his own thinking, as quoted, where Aristotle grounds education, the teaching of infants, the birth of civilization, in the ordering of shit. This was precisely the kind of barren anti-philosophy that the man before me, the dead man before me, was once capable of. He and I were connected, I have to admit, we knew each other since we were children. And I did have some fondness for the man, but it evaporated at work when he came walking in with his theories and ideas that he wished to press upon me but that I had no time for, naturally, given the requirements of my job, the pressures of it, and the high intellectual standards some of us still attempt to uphold. I remembered now where I had heard this argument before. I had not paid attention, or all that much attention, when, years ago, he came rushing in to tell me and those I stood with at the time that *meconium*, the shit of the new-born, was absolutely at the core of his argument, like a perfect substance, he said, in which all its dimensions overlapped (the dimensions of his argument), so that meconium was both at the root of his thought and his great revelation. In *meconium* the entire edifice of Western civilisation unravels, he said to us. Education originates in shit and it resembles an intoxicant. No, he corrected himself, it *is* an intoxicant. Education, he said, is driven toward the production of waste, education takes the fabric of life and tears it up and shits it out, he told us as we stood about not quite sure what to do, though my colleagues looked to me, expectantly. Since I knew him, I should deal with him, he was my responsibility, it was up to me to do it, and so I did, taking his arm to usher him toward my office, but then, at the crucial moment, down a back passage that led out of the building, avoiding the main stairway, the foyer, other colleagues, and somehow rid myself of the man by making some kind of promise to attend, more closely, at a better and more opportune time, to the extremely significant remarks he had just made, a time when I would be better able, more easily disposed, to giving them the attention they deserved. Assuredly they had struck me as *portentous* remarks, I used words like that to soothe him, remarks that should not be considered lightly, I continued, and not without preparation. These remarks deserved full, sustained attention that my mind, which I apologised for, was not yet able to devote, it was clouded with the pressures of work, and so really what we needed was to set aside some time. With the others, he asked. Yes, I replied, most definitely. A seminar, I suggested, specially convened, I added. Just leave it with me, I said, or said something like that, and patted him on his back which was more of a push in the direction of the street. Sitting now before his silent body, and having finally read the opening words of the book of pages his son gave me, I had some sense of what he meant that day, years ago, as he strained the limits of our friendship. It was a regular imposition, this was not the first interruption or his last, but one of many, frequent interruptions. It was because of our shared history, the history my family had with his, a connection between us and our respective families which was purely non-professional and had no place at work, or at least not like this, as my colleagues paused with me to bear the intrusion. We were, we had once been, Christian Scientists. Our families were bound together by that religion, the religion that brought us up and warped our minds and made us what we were, even though I escaped my upbringing and he did not. Whereas I made a break with the religion that brought us up, he remained trapped by it. Whereas I entirely escaped the grasp of that religion and became an independent being, a thinking, reasoning being, he was trapped by that religion for the rest of his life, even though he was no longer a formal member of that Church, and had only been trapped by it, in a household that observed it, as a young boy. Even though he was a Christian Scientist and had been subject to a Christian Science upbringing for just a few years, only his first years, he remained marked by that religion for the rest of his life, deranged by it, as I was not. The religion that deranged him did not affect me. I observed it from a distance and noticed how its deranged teachings— *sickness is illusion, death is illusion, the body does not exist*—continued to influence him, even though he had nothing to do with the Church, even though no surviving members of his family were still in it, even though none existed who were known to him who had not renounced it. He and I were bound together not simply by our shared childhood, but by the religion that destroyed him and which I escaped. He visited me at work because of it. When he walked down the corridor and sought me out, he was still trailing the effects of that religion, much to my embarrassment. My colleagues had no idea. They were merely aware of a connection, of some sort, that bound him to me. They did not enquire about the nature of our connection. Fortunately, they considered such questions impolite, or so I gathered, and did not interrogate me about him. They did not ask why he trailed me. But they did expect me to deal with him. We stood there, my colleagues and I, deep in conversation regarding something of considerable significance, of great intellectual importance and subtlety no doubt, and found ourselves interrupted by him as he entered our circle with the word *meconium* on his lips. He reacted to his upbringing—its denial of the body—by insisting on the body. When he bombarded us with this word *meconium*, he was actually just insisting on the body, the body and its waste which his religion rejected as illusion. When he went on and on about faecal matter, all he was doing was pointing to the body that produced it. He was responding to the religion that first brought him up, that told him the body does not exist, in the most infantile way, by saying, look here, look here is some caca, here is my doo-doo, look now, my body made this. I recall him saying that time he interrupted us at work, *It will be the epigraph of my book.* This word *meconium* will be the epigraph, he repeated, and we wondered, and they looked at me, and I looked at him and thought, you must go. I will lead you away and dispose of you down the back passage of our offices, I thought. I will make you think that you are coming to my office and then, at the crucial moment, I will take a turn and dispose of you onto the street. The kindest thing I can do to you right now, I thought, is dispose of you like that. Otherwise, my colleagues will simply look at you, and then look at me, and continue to think about the epigraph you just mentioned and realise with ever greater certainty that your honorary lectureship was a mistake. They will look at you and question your existence, I thought, but then they will look at me and question mine. And here it is, that epigraph, on another page that eased itself out of the pile as if delivering that memory of his interruption, and my embarrassment, onto my lap. **Meconium** (*n.*) *The first shit of the newly born child, composed of materials ingested in the uterus: mucus, bile, amniotic fluid, skin cells, etc. From the Latin, 'poppy-like,' derived from the Greek given its resemblance to raw opium.* This is where the epigraph ended, which was hardly appropriate for an epigraph, I thought, being a mere definition. Its placement at the beginning of this manuscript was clearly of great significance to him who later wrote, on a subsequent page, *The association with raw opium is telling.* From birth, he continued, the child submits to an educational gaze that finds itself addicted to the shit it curates. Ridiculous nonsense, I thought. Addicted to shit? Meconium shit? The association with opium, here, by him, was a perfect example of his tendency to overreach himself, to blend ideas without any attention to the distance between them and thereby produce ridiculous amalgams of thought which poured out much like the shit he saw, or claimed to see, everywhere about him. This was a perfect example of the notion, I thought, and I know it isn't that simple, which states that all philosophies are effectively confessions betraying the condition and outlook of their author. His condition was poor, and so his outlook was poor. This work, these pages, were the product of that poor outlook. He had an impoverished view of the world, and that viewpoint infected his thought and his writing. His life was diminished, and so his outlook was diminished. His Church had maimed him, and so his thought was destroyed. And there I was reading it despite myself due to my confinement in the front room, trapped in that room with those pages, sat opposite his son. Education, he continued, becomes intoxicated by the enormity of what it must achieve in order to rescue the child from the mute stupidity of its amniotic sac. *Mute stupidity of its amniotic sac.* This statement hardly made any sense to me. The child arrives in the world, he continued, trapped within a body it cannot command, the experience of which can only become a matter of communication long after it has submitted to the word, to knowledge, inspection, and rule. Only once the body has been ordered and thus domesticated, or at least half domesticated and half ordered, can the experience of the body be conveyed. That hardly lessened my confusion. Only after the experience of the body once directly felt in its incontrollable excess has been diminished by the organising mechanisms of a basically ruthless educational imposition, only once the experience of the body has been lost, in large part, from the agencies of perception, can its story be told and the meaning of its presence be rendered intelligible. I gave up. These were precisely the kind of pseudo-intellectual remarks we hated him for. This was a perfect example of the type of intellectual masquerade that gives the rest of us a bad name. Remarks such as these actively damaged the intellectual reputations of those such as myself who use similar concepts, but do so in a manner that is respectable, and properly thought out, whereas his work was produced, so I felt, in imitation of ours, and demonstrated a superficial understanding of the serious intellectual foundations upon which our remarks and arguments were built. I had once thought words resembling his, and made similar points, but I had written it all up in a more respectable way which placed my arguments completely at odds with his. Whereas our ideas were published in the most distinguished journals, his ideas remained unpublished and virtually unpublishable. Whereas our ideas extended the work of the intellect, his ideas made a mockery of the intellectual life. When it comes to the body, he went on, education is both the agent and the product of a basic forgetfulness. The body is trained by education, and this is how the body is forgotten. We forget that our bodies are not within our command, he wrote. Our bodies rebel at every moment, *with each peristaltic motion*, he actually wrote that, *with each peristaltic motion* the body motions its rebellion, *but education refuses every quiet reflex*, he continued. Education declares that the body will be ruled, which is another way of saying, the body must submit. But the great reveal is at birth itself, he continued. He was absolutely sure, I could see, that his brief study of birth would unravel the West. This study will unravel the West, I could hear him say. My argument about birth will take the rug from under Western thought. My argument will reveal the West to itself and cause it to finally annihilate itself and abort anyone who might still feel the effects of its legacy. The West will only linger on just long enough to annihilate anyone influenced by it, he would say, as if he were the first to truly perceive its malice, as if no other thinker had ever held the West in contempt. Birth and the first days thereafter, he wrote, are experienced with great intensity but through a veil of misunderstanding and forgetfulness. This, he wrote, explains the intoxicating effects of the new-born. There is a determination on behalf of spectators and handlers to avoid the horror of the child, an inchoate mass of energies, a creature overcome with desire and want. At birth, educated people, by which I mean Westerners, he added, have the ability to see a new-born and at the same time not see the new-born. This takes place in the delirium they create, under which these intoxicated spectators exude the call of domestication which the wretched little creature, just emerged, already rebels against as it generates chaos, as it appears in all its great unreasonableness. Small children are unreasonable, unreasoning miscreants, he wrote, and the function of education and culture—however friendly to the life of the child they may seem—is to destroy their rebellion and teach submission. The hatefulness of each new-born from the perspective of culture and reason would be seen in its full abysmal alterity, he wrote, if children did not function at the same time as intoxicants. The smell of the child. The sound of its breath. The fur on its shoulders. I had no idea there would be fur on my son's shoulders, he wrote, but I loved it outright, as he once told me, and did so even before a nurse told him it was perfectly normal, and the fur would fall off soon enough, and he did not after all have a son who was innately furry. This was merely womb fur, as he called it, and not permanent fur as it first seemed. Even the stench. These all serve to intoxicate, thankfully, necessarily, but at the cost of a great misunderstanding, he wrote. Just listen to the sound of an adult in the presence of a new-born, the nonsense adults are reduced to. Adults rehearse that sound before dogs and cats often enough. Listen to an adult before a dog, or a cat, worse still a puppy, or a kitten, and hear the drivel adults indulge themselves in. Westerners use their dogs and cats to coo over in order to rehearse the idiocies they emit before children. These responses are all signs of their intoxication. The new-born child can only be experienced by those who engage it, by those who welcome it, in a state of delirium. New-born children can only be survived by their parents if their parents are reduced to a state of abject idiocy in their presence. The child can only be received into the world and welcomed by delirious adults, he wrote. This does not last, he added. Gradually the intoxicating smell of the child diminishes as the production of chaos continues. The child generates that chaos by having no sense of remorse, no proper feeling for the consequences of its actions, or if the child has some sense, or some feeling, both sense and feeling remain underdeveloped and therefore cannot count as sense or feeling in the proper sense. The child fails for its first years to feel the true purchases of guilt and causes pain in others almost involuntarily and without much deviant insight or design. The child adheres, initially and always, to the basic typology of the stunted sadist. Small children are basically stunted sadists, he wrote, although none will call them that. Even when the small child no longer intoxicates like the new-born once did and so becomes irritating to those around it, the word sadist will not be used and will strike anyone who hears it as excessive and inhuman. And yet, the passage from birth to early childhood can be measured by the growing irritation of those who must care for the developing child. There is no better way, he wrote, of measuring child development. To measure child development merely develop a test for the growing irritation of those who care for the child, who are forced to spend time with the child and submit to the whims, the rebellions, the multiple unreasonable events of childhood. The smell of the child, once experienced like a drug, inhaled deeply, finally diminishes, though not in a manner that allows at last for the child to be recognised as another impossible organism made of desire and pain and want, rather, the smell of the child gives way before the greatest intoxicant of all, the call to educate, he wrote, which covers the, by now, bad or at least not quite so alluring scent of the developing child, replacing it with the reeking musk of educational commitment. The call to educate intoxicates and dulls perception for those who would otherwise suffer worse, that is to say more than usual, when faced with the irritating presence of the child, with the persistent unreasonableness of childhood. The child would destroy all those who come into contact with it, if not for the fact that most children can be educated, are brought to civilization, and thereby driven out of themselves into the very different unreasonableness of adulthood. This call to educate is presumed ancient, as old as civilized life, he wrote. And the call to educate *does have a history*, he added with emphasis. But that history, such as may be, is one we retrospectively construct, he wrote. It helps give seriousness to a purpose, to the great mission of civilised, educated existence, that must exceed us and against which we must always be measured poorly, he wrote. Even noble efforts to educate others, and educate the self, will remain failed attempts to realise the promise of educational fulfilment in its full unattainable glory. Educated culture is built that way. Education never delivers, he wrote, not truly. It always withholds its promise. And still we are accustomed to claiming that education and educated culture can be rescued even as it is being debased, everywhere reduced to the lowest version of itself. A vision of education, he went on, figured now as a culture of fulfilment, enrichment, depth, tolerance, and so on, helps distinguish between education in the higher sense and education in its reduced instrumentalised form, the failing school, the school that has forgotten its mission, the school that begins to overtly brutalise its children. At their worst these schools are mere exam factories, as they say, or prisons, nothing more than holding pens to allow adults to go to work and be exploited there in turn. These schools represent the lowest form of education, we like to think, he wrote, or some think, he added, given that many people are still largely content with their schools if they favour their children with success. But this rejection of the school in its diminished, modern form, he wrote, and its association with *The Machine*, is too easy, he added. Schooling in the modern sense would not exist or survive without the dignity of education, without the shadow that the assumed greatness of education casts on all lower forms. We only admire schools, or at least tolerate them, because we admire ourselves as schooled beings. That assumed superiority is the reason for the unrelenting stupidity of our age, he wrote. The stupidity of our age, he went on, is its profound inability to see just how far the rot spreads, how deeply all good intentions, all higher thoughts, are implicated in everything, in every catastrophe that this age, our great age of universalised education claims to abhor. The self-given status of educated people, that is to say, of cultured people, of theatre goers, art gallery visitors, museum members, food aficionados, and so on, standing erect before their own conceit, causes that shadow, he wrote, referring here to the shadow of educational greatness he had just invoked. It is our shadow, he added. This great shadow is produced as we stand on the verge of annihilation. The sun is on its way down. This shadow is long, elongated, malformed. It is a grotesque shadow, he continued, but we still mistake as if it were the sign of something higher, as if it signalled the intrinsic greatness of our kind, the greatness of those who still appreciate culture, philosophy, science, art, and intellect. Those who can still appreciate such things do so despite all evidence, despite the obvious failure of their very objects of attachment, that is, despite the failure of culture, philosophy, science, art, and intellect to prevent the coming apocalypse, which, very probably, they have also helped cause. I paused. These lines were familiar to me, or the gist of it. I remember him saying something similar on the walk we took south of the city last winter, about how our shadows were longer than we deserved, that we believed too much in the importance of our intellects and the depths of our conversation, even though I, as I listened to these words, found myself wishing that this particular conversation would draw to a close. His version of the intellect bore no relation to my own. Whereas I upheld the intellect, he travestied it. I hardly listened or tried not to.

We crossed the fields, stone walls, and gates. There were some sheep, but it was mainly vacant grass and field thistles, and I remember thinking as we passed a ruin in one of those fields that I would rather go into that ruin than listen to him talk. The ruin was completely uninteresting, probably just a shepherd's hut, but I had a strong desire to walk away from him and his incessant talk and begin inspecting it. Now, sitting here, I had no hope of doing so. There was no chance of returning to that ruin, of walking through those exact fields, past the very thistles I avoided that day, and of finally entering it. It was, after all, his route that we took, the idea of a walk was his suggestion too, I was not quite sure I could retrace it having paid little attention to the ways and turns of our passage through that region as I laboured on beside him, following him, lamenting him, abusing him in my mind for destroying an otherwise pleasant walk with the words and ideas he shared, since I was, on that walk, unable to escape or duck out of our conversation as is my habit. Usually he barely managed a sentence or two before I found some excuse for leaving him standing, or sitting, due to some urgent commitment or unavoidable distraction which really I had no control over, so I said, and had to submit to, I added, despite the urgency if not desperation in his eyes which told of his great need to be heard, a need that I could not answer, because it pained me to listen just as much as it pained him to be dismissed, ignored, and downtrodden by my indifference if not distaste for his work and thought, which all my colleagues shared, which all people shared, at some basic level, when he opened his mouth. The mechanisms which generate the assumed dignity, of intellect, of serious conversation, I read, are created in the moment. The mechanisms which produce the so-called depth and importance we associate with education and the bearing of educated people, which attract us to one another and allow us to recognise each other as peers, as people we are prepared to listen to, and take seriously, and rate, he wrote, have been long in construction, but the basis of dignity itself is not ancient at all. It is not necessary to bang on about Cicero, or repeat Shakespeare, in order to be an educated person. The educated person is just a set of gestures, a system of manners and conceits, a set of cultural reflexes. The educated person looks and sounds like an educated person, and so they are. We perceive dignity, and so it appears. I sighed. There was something totemic and distinctly if not manically obsessive about his preoccupation with education and educated people, as if this were the basic problem, the fundamental existential problem, and not in actual fact a contrived problem, essentially a non-problem which he had constructed for himself, a problem that met and satisfied his diminished outlook on life, and so did something for him, if only in a negative sense, but had nothing to offer others, and held no broader significance beyond the limitations of his under-stimulated—he would like to think over-stimulated—state of mind. Education is a present-day notion, he wrote. The dignity of education, of what it means to be educated, is a resolute and repeated fabrication born of hubris, hackneyed technique, and not a little greed. Acquisitive, assuredly, in it for the self and dismissive of all others, education is a product of our desperate, grasping present. Etcetera. And so on. Bombast, I thought. I put this particular page back down on the stack and looked up. The son was still in a kind of sleep, his eyes fluttering so that I felt both alone in my consciousness but also, quite possibly, observed. I thought again of the ruin. If it were not for the history our family shared I would not have been there with him, on that walk, walking with a man I had once played with as a child and tolerated even then because our parents insisted we spend time together. This was before I was sent away to school at eleven, a school his parents would not be enticed to pay for, but it was not his time anyway. He was three years younger than me, not quite making his eighth birthday before I left. At seven he was unusually gullible, I remember, or at least trusting, so that I could plan around him and if necessary free myself of him, something I repeatedly did at the old mineshaft near where we lived but not so near that our parents knew of its existence, or close enough that they might hear us, or hear him to be precise, a trick he always fell for as I persuaded him to go down, saying that yes I would follow, even though I only planned to pull the rope back up behind him, of course, and retreat to a good distance out of earshot for a bit of peace. I would sit and wait it out. By the time I returned he was so desperately grateful and at the same time introverted as a consequence of his terror, that the effect of peace and quiet for me lasted until we arrived back at his house, or my own. I went down a mine once as an adult. It was not all that long ago. I was making my way along the beach of an island not far from here, a day's travel. The opening to the mine was above, in the cliff. This was not something I had ever seen before, an entrance to a mine in the face of a cliff, where this entrance was some way over head height and out of which hung a knotted rope. I hauled myself up. Once inside and after I had gone a little way, crawling due to the low ceiling, observing the decaying props, wondering if this was a bad idea, it occurred to me that what I did to him as a child might be described as cruel, although all children are cruel to one another, I thought, and I did just as often if not more often go down with him into the mine, holding the rope as he descended. Down there we went as far as we dared which probably wasn't that far at all. I did look after him and keep him safe, it was a place where a child might easily disappear, unexpected holes, internal mineshafts down which you could drop, and which I pointed out with me being the older boy, older and more perceptive of danger, so that my attitude was actually of a caring sort, or at least I wanted to avoid him killing himself by some accident, which would have been traumatic for me too, all the explaining I would have to do as I imagined making my way out and facing my parents, his parents, an enquiry most probably, and all the attention of a kind that most children that age would rather not attract. And then the mine would be closed off too once they had retrieved him, which would be a shame. As a child he was plagued at times, I remember, with morbid thoughts, he even called them that. He went on and on about these morbid thoughts, about death, his own, which he would tell me about and I found odd, being not myself preoccupied by such things, or hardly not, and so finding myself unable to fully or even partly empathise with the terror that he spoke of or tried to explain. It was as if something like a great cavern opened up inside him, that is how he put it, around the chest or stomach thereabouts, and began to pull him inward. He felt it in his throat, drawing down not only himself but dragging at all he perceived about him as if the entire universe as he knew it, or felt it, would gather up with his innards and fall into oblivion. It would fall into such a high state of compression that everything became a supremely massed point, he said, all matter existing in one place for a moment, a singularity of his making, before it vanished with him, and for which he was ultimately responsible, a responsibility he felt with more weight than anyone could imagine, even though it was also inevitable, he knew, as inevitable as death that this should happen to him, and that all he felt, and all that existed around him, would become nothing. He could not understand, he told me, why others were not all feeling the same pull all of the time, or at least some of the time, because as he looked about him he didn't see others suffering as he sometimes felt, and that confused him, and helped confirm his first suspicion that surely he was alone in his uniqueness, and his consciousness was something alone in the universe, and could not die, unlike everyone else. I cannot die because *I am me*, he said, which just made the thought of death even more terrible and brought the weight of things into that point, to the cavern as he called it, with greater force. He would arrive at his sister's bedroom some nights, he told me, and tell her of his fear, of the abysmal feeling inside him that was his realisation of the certainty of death. There was nothing she could say against a feeling like that. He knew that he would die, and felt it acutely, and was at the same time certain it should never happen. He felt his entire organism refuse the prospect, his very being declared against the certainty of death. It tore at him, this feeling. His death, he told me, was as unthinkable as it was unique from all other deaths, though he knew, of course, that people died all the time and there had been countless deaths before him and dying was easy and nothing was more assured than his own death, or banal, but still, he could not shake the feeling that death, for him, was impossible, and that if he died it would be no ordinary death and so it couldn't happen. This, at least, is how I remember him describing that feeling, his terror, his incredulity, although surely he used different words to express how he felt, and perhaps I still have no real idea what he was attempting to explain to me in those conversations which I hated, partly because they bored me, or, to use a word I would not have then used, because they struck me as profoundly narcissistic. His preoccupation with his own death sealed him off from all the death around him. It was a vulgar self-obsession and I hated him for it. I cannot believe now that he was not quite eight at the time and have begun to wonder if this was a later memory, perhaps from one of my visits home during the holidays from school, before his mother moved away, that is, after which we no longer saw one another, not even during the holiday period. As a younger child he was definitely odd in a similar way as if his oddness were a precursor to his later thought, or non-thought as I liked to think of it. I think his parents never saw it. In their company he was the perfect child, quiet and submissive in the presence of family and friends from The Church of Christ, Scientist, our common religion, most would call it a sect. Not even my parents, who were already at the periphery of the Church, did see it. After all, in the contexts of that religion we did not speak of death since death did not exist for us. There is no death in The Church of Christ, Scientist. At worst its members *passed on*, as the euphemism went, because death was inadmissible. This did not strike me then, as it strikes me now, as an absurd and dangerous teaching. Back then it was just another lesson to absorb. Death was a material illusion that the Church taught against. Once I left, when he was still only eight and I was eleven, his circumstances changed. His father died and then his mother left the Church. She came to hold the Church responsible for her husband's early death, and eventually moved away and remarried into the ordinary religion which brought her son up as a teenager. This was the religion of the family setting in which I now sat, and would be the religion to bury him and not cremate him as The Church of Christ, Scientist disposed of its members. I cannot for the life of me understand the point of that comma before the word Scientist. It has always perplexed me though I never asked about it. The Church of Christ, Scientist always appeared written like that with the comma. We were both still influenced, I felt, by our early upbringing in The Church of Christ, Scientist, which, in its teachings, denied the existence of the body too, and the existence of sickness, just as it denied the reality of death. I was surely still influenced by that upbringing although I could not identify where exactly it still affected me. Psychically, maybe. Perhaps having some shaping effect on my character, but surely there was no effect on my work and thought, or my professional life, most of all my intellectual life. I like to think that in all the important areas I have entirely escaped the influence of my upbringing. I could see that his upbringing was foregrounded in his own writing and thought, that it influenced his thought in a way it did not so clearly influence mine, if at all, given his persistent obsession with death, for instance, and his preoccupation with sickness, obvious preoccupations about which he had burdened me on more than one occasion, and then with all he wrote and thought about the body and its denial. All his thought was, in the end, nothing but a mere counterargument to the denial of the body, to the refusal of its material existence, which forms one of the fundamental tenets of The Church of Christ, Scientist. This was a basic tenet that he rejected, turned from, and turned against as a young man, and then continued to oppose as an older man, never able to escape or develop beyond its conditioning effects. It was clear to me that The Church of Christ, Scientist was still dominating his thought, as if it were still his religion, if not consciously, but as something he still needed to resist even though he was no longer a member of that Church and a member of its community but had been freed of it from an early age due to the decision of his mother who finally came to see that the religion she, herself, had been brought into was, for her, an abhorrent religion that destroyed lives, that, by its beliefs, caused the death of its members by refusing them access to doctors, to medicine, by convincing them as it did that they would only heal themselves by denying the fact that they were ill, sick, diseased, and suffering, as if that denial of the body, of death, sickness, and so on, would save them, although in the end it only killed them like it killed his father and as it surely killed other fathers, sons, daughters, and mothers too, as so many have testified. It is no exaggeration to point out that The Church of Christ, Scientist is actually followed not so much—or not only—by its faithful, but is trailed to a greater extent by a considerable tally of unnecessary and preventable death. All he did, and all his life amounted to, I felt, was an attempt to write against the religion that his mother rejected, writing needlessly, since she rejected it for his benefit as well as her own, and did so successfully, a decisive act, a bold and courageous act which was her achievement, not his, so that everything he later achieved in writing and thought was a mere repetition of what his mother had already done on his behalf when he was a child. All that he wrote he need not have written, or bothered thinking, since his mother had already done it for him. His thought, everything he believed he had achieved, merely recapitulated his mother's turn against The Church of Christ, Scientist following the death of his father. All he managed was to repeat her turn against the Church, but without the same courage, or need, doing as his mother did but doing it badly, a miserable imitator of some events he witnessed as a child following the death of his father, and that he never left behind him. He saw her act courageously, but he never understood what courage was. He was trapped by his need to do as his mother had done, to feel as his mother did. She rejected the Church and I always admired her for it. He rejected nothing. He spent the rest of his life looking for something and pretending to reject it when she had already rejected it all for him. I know that it is usually considered reductive, insulting to the intelligence, if not also a sign of intellectual laziness, to accuse others of merely reflecting in thought their prior experience, and I am no follower of Freud, or the so-called Freudian influence, or the Freudian tendency, or whatever, even unwittingly. I actually have no taste for Freud, not even distaste. When it comes to Freud I am entirely neutral so that when I refuse Freud I do so almost acciden- tally as an after-effect of my neutrality in relation to Freud and the so-called Freudian tendency, but in this case, I thought, it was pain- fully obvious that most of what he actually managed to think in later life, his non-thought, was simply an extension of what he experi- enced as a child, as if he never escaped his childhood. Even though he dressed up his thought by imitating mine and so obscured, if only a little, and to those who did not know him as I did, the origins of his thought in his childhood, it was clear enough to me that his thought was the expression of his intellectual imprisonment. His imprison- ment extended from his earliest memories to the last things he said and wrote, some of which now sat on my lap, and which his son, who clearly revered his father, now dead, felt I should do something with, since there was, for the son, a clear affinity between his father's writing and mine, his father's thought and my thought, and thus—so his reasoning went—I was ideally placed to give his father an intellec- tual afterlife, the kind of posterity his son believed he deserved and that I found awkward, if not repellent, since I knew that his thought and his writing deserved nothing of the sort, given that it had no sig- nificance beyond the limits of his experience. He only railed against the intellect and the life of educated people because he was brought up in a religion that was basically anti-intellectual. He thought that he refused his first religion, but in actual fact he only fulfilled it by continuing its work as an anti-intellectual, anti-modern sect. His son expected me to make something of this manuscript, but it was basically an anti-intellectual tract. There was no way of responding to it on an intellectual level without tearing it apart. I was invited to this wake under that pretext. I was brought here based on a complete misunderstanding. I was wanted as a thinker and a writer, even though the son, and the father, had no idea what it took to think and to write. My proof, as I told myself, was the experiment I had performed on an annual basis for four years now, although it did not begin as an experiment, and probably was not repeated exclusively as an experiment but was first done out of distaste for the man before me and remained driven year on year by that distaste until he died. This experiment, which was not intended as such, or not initially, demonstrated to me that his thought did not represent the process of discovery by which proper intellects work, or so I felt, a process of intellectual creation that involves some measure of inspiration and unrepeatable chance, and effort of course, but was in this case the direct consequence of his prior experience which he drew on, unwittingly, and expressed in his writing, so that when he appeared to write about things of broader existential significance, all he did was express some psychic mechanism and organisation of his innards, transforming them into words that surrounded him and said nothing profound beyond his experience, or nothing extendable to others, and conveyed nothing more than his unique and diminished perspective, the outlook of a man who has never and will never see beyond the limitations of his own formative imprisonment. His thought, his writing, only testified to his failure in both domains, his failure to think, and his failure to write. He arrived at our annual conference, and being unable to secure a presentation-slot, stood up and delivered the very talk that the organising committee had rejected, having denied him a slot to speak at that conference, as is common practice, a denial he surely deserved since there must be some measure of quality and a degree of gatekeeping in order for a conference to sustain itself as an intellectually respectable entity. He presented his rejected paper, illegally then, from the audience or the floor as it is sometimes called, with the speaker whose slot he was occupying sitting on stage and peering down at him, completely appalled as was his right. I was also in the audience and soon enough everybody looked at me, they scarcely even looked at him, I am not sure if they looked at him at all but turned to me insistently, since he was my responsibility, our family had a shared history, he and I had a personal connection, and so surely I would do something about his interruption, although, as I knew, there was nothing I could do. He considered that he had a right to be there as a member of the audience due to his honorary position, a right he exploited, and now that he was in full flow I knew he would not listen to me, even though they all felt he might, that he would respond to me better than anyone and be persuaded to leave, or at least stop. He would, I was sure, not even see me if I stood before him and pleaded with him to leave and give the audience a break. So, we endured it, many walked out, but I and a few others somehow stayed on. The speaker on stage eventually went to find another room, with some following him, others dispersing elsewhere, grumbling, and complaining, and rightfully so. Two delegates did attempt to forcibly remove him once it became clear that I would do nothing to stop it, but they were not prepared in the end to actually manhandle him out of the room. He did not yield as they first attempted, as a kind of prompt, to hold him by the upper arms as if that would do to move him on. Once he finished his talk, only I was left, trapped with my anger, embarrassed by my association with the man if not compromised professionally by our connection, since what he'd said had sounded a little like what I might say, though it was obvious to me and surely obvious to anyone who knew my work, and had any discernment, that there was no relation between us at all, on the intellectual side. He finally looked at me, gave me a nod, and then went out, after which I followed him, eventually, to the foyer where he stood alone, where others stood too, but in groups, making small-talk, exchanging professional niceties and bits of gossip with the odd glance and gesture at the man who now held a small coffee in one hand and his brown leather case in the other, in which he had deposited his notes, a great pile of pages, some of which he had read and the rest of which represented his thought up until that point, as he had told us, referring to his notes as he talked from the floor and as the rest of us looked on appalled. I watched him stand and sip his coffee as if he did not sense his isolation, sipping his coffee, regarding it, and looking ponderously across the foyer to nothing in particular, so far as I could tell, standing, taking another sip, and pondering, holding his coffee, then sipping it again, as if it was a perfectly ordinary moment and he had not after all disgraced himself and insulted me by association, not simply by the interruption, which floored everyone, but intellectually, given what he said and how he made his pronouncements, as if what he had to say held world-historical importance, though really it displayed, in its very confidence and the self-assured manner he adopted, a degree of stupidity, a kind of obliviousness, that matched the near-unimaginable arrogance of what he had just done. I found that brown leather case on his desk some days later when I happened to be visiting to pick up some post that he had, quite unnecessarily, picked up for me when he was last at the department. I took the stack of pages it contained and made off with them in my own bag, including the post, some letters, and a book just published by an esteemed colleague that I had been sent to review, returning home with the collection of papers, the summation of his thought as he had called it, and dumped the whole lot, his papers, not the post, in the back garden near some old and decaying vegetables including the pumpkin my daughter had planted, and I had neglected, which might seem a shame, although anyone who has not seen a pumpkin rot has no conception of how strangely a rancid pumpkin descends into the ground. It liquifies inwardly at first, imperceptibly so, held together only by the skin, the lower part begins to collapse with the upper half still holding its shape, and so it goes, by degrees until there is nothing left but slurry. This year I watched the event for the first time, sitting nearby when the weather was still good with a manuscript by another esteemed colleague that I was presently reviewing. Each time I sat there the pumpkin was a bit worse off. Behind the pumpkin a pile of weeds, themselves rotting, were mixed in with a few kitchen scraps added when I was about and remembered to do it, peelings and so on, teabags, and sometimes the stuff that collects in the trap of the kitchen sink. The potato skins were sprouting. So not quite a compost. To make it worse I had thrown some branches in at some point that were too big to rot, at least not for a while, and had screwed up the entire operation by doing that, and being too distracted, really, by my work, had not sorted it out, but gave up, throwing on more scraps when I could be bothered for that although most of the kitchen waste went with everything else to landfill, or the incinerator, or wherever rubbish goes in this city. This is how I go about it in the garden, hacking back sections every so often and then forgetting about those parts of the garden until the hacking back becomes necessary again, which I think is understandable given that my natural home is an intellectual one and so the garden is only a distraction. My daughter offered to sort it out, but I told her not to bother. To stop the stack from blowing about I decided to piss all over it as much as I could. I was reluctant to bring his manuscript into the house which is why I was here, pissing now on the lot of it. The bin was not a good idea. It was out on the street by the front wall. I never bring it in. But then it occurred to me that the pages in the garden might attract attention from the house if he visited, and so I turned them over with a fork, together with the stuff underneath, and then added a few more branches torn from a nearby bush that had over-grown and that I had not yet found the time to do anything about. It started to rain and I returned inside, glad of the rain to augment the piss. I avoided him successfully for two weeks after that, so that when we next met, he had moved on from what would have been a few frantic days of searching. He told me about his loss, and I nodded, and thought about the piss, and then explained to me in some detail that the loss, his loss, was a loss not just for himself but was a loss for his peers, those such as myself, who must surely understand its signifi-cance, and a loss for his broader audience too, an audience not yet assembled, he knew, and which had not yet encountered his work but would one day gather and finally understand the importance of what he had written and thought. As he explained this to me with a coffee in my hand, I thought, drinking that coffee, how there was no retrieving his manuscript from the slurry. He spent the next eleven and a half months reassembling his thought, as he put it, reproducing what he had lost, all the ideas, all the key claims, even attempting to use the same phraseology and paragraph structure, the same sentences and word choices, even the same punctuation, he said, since the manner in which he expressed his ideas was key to their meaning, a point that caused me some considerable irritation given the extent to which I felt his writing imitated the kind of language, the conceptual terms I and my peers adopted to express our thought. It was not as if he had nothing else to do. He still had two children who could not understand when they were small, and tried to understand when they were older, why he spent so much time writing, spending all that time alone, and not with them, although they could not know the full absurdity of it, as I knew, that what he did amounted to very little and that he had the respect of no one. Given the extent to which his work resembled the work of people such as myself, so that to the untrained eye it had a similar status, his children felt, as they grew older, that his diligent preoccupation with writing, and the fact that from their earliest memories he sat alone when he might have been with them, a fact they combined with their knowledge of his honorary position and his frequent visits to the faculty where I worked, explained why he spent so much time away from them, even as he lived with them, stealing every minute he could to assemble his great project in thought. But as anyone who has ever created something original or at least distinct in thought and writing must know, the process of creation cannot be repeated. Even every interruption has a role, since each interruption helps put off the act of creation in thought to the right moment, as I have often felt, to the precise configuration of accidents and habits that produce the artefact that the thinker, or the artist, looks back on and considers an event in thought and history that could not have occurred otherwise and could never be repeated. Whenever I have lost work, due to some malfunction in the machine I have been using, I have experienced that loss as a great trauma, knowing that there is no repeating what has gone, and that all I can do is gather together the thoughts I can still recall and turn them into something else. The loss of his papers should have been irreparable, something he could not remedy and would never reassemble, at least not in that form as he hoped, word for word, phrase for phrase, and paragraph after paragraph, which is how he put it. I hardly believed he actually achieved what he claimed to have done as he returned to the conference in its next year with another stack of papers that, he claimed, were a near perfect reproduction of the papers he had lost, that I had taken and disposed of, although the fact he hoped to reproduce what he could never have reproduced without a photographic memory, or some other aid, demonstrated to me that he had no conception of the process of intellectual creation, and had no notion of what it means to take thought into new realms, to travel with thought beyond the limitations of experience. This merely confirmed my strong conviction that all he thought and wrote was a mere extension of his childhood experience, not in any Freudian sense, I have no taste or distaste for Freud. His thought just extended his childhood experience on an intellectual plane, and reflected, without exceeding it, the original limitations of his perspective, his imprisonment, so that what he produced after eleven and a half months was not a literal copy of what he had lost, but reflected, by some reflex arc, the diminished perspective he could not escape, though he pretended to, as he adopted my idiom, took my phraseology, and made claims that presented themselves as existential discoveries of world-historical importance. He stood up like he had done a year before and delivered his talk. It did sound familiar though it could not have been identical to the talk he last gave from the audience, from which almost everyone fled, apart from myself and a couple of others. There was an additional section to his talk, however, a new introduction of sorts in which he explained that almost a year ago he had somehow lost his entire life's work, which was the culmination of his thought up until that point, a considerable loss, he said, given that he was now getting on in years. He had spent the last eleven or so months working to reconstruct his life's work, from memory, *word for word*, he said with emphasis. And it was because of this loss and the time it had taken him to reassemble his thought that he had not had the opportunity to think anything new over the last few months given just how much he had to reassemble, which was again why, in contravention to the usual conference expectation that new and original work should be presented, he would again be presenting a similar talk to last year, for which he asked our indulgence—only three of us were left by that point—although it was unavoidable that he should be in this position, he said, given the scale of his loss and the size of the task he had faced in stitching it all back together. As he went on, my irritation, my understandable, entirely justifiable irritation, was accompanied by the thought that I should probably test his claim to reproduce his words, *word for word*, even though I doubted that claim of course, and it was almost a foregone conclusion he could not actually rewrite the manuscript I had destroyed word for word as he said. Still, it would be interesting to see just how close he came to reproducing it that way, since this would demonstrate the extent to which his thought was the unthinking consequence of his childhood experience. It would show his imprisonment, his continued entrapment by an influence he could not escape, evidently, and that was clearly the basis for so much of what he produced. I could not imagine that he would reproduce his so-called great work from memory, but I did think that any subsequent sections of text which did bear close relation to what he had originally written would surely represent the least original, most diminished side of his intellect. Anything he did manage to reproduce, exactly written, would be a mere extension of his childhood experience, a trace of his conditioning. As I observed him later in the foyer, standing just like he did the year before, with a coffee in one hand and his brown leather case in the other, sipping his coffee, looking ahead, apparently oblivious to those about him who were talking to one another and would look over, on occasion, as he sipped his coffee, and gesture towards the man with something like derision, if not disdain, before returning—as he continued to sip—to the usual chat that goes for intellectual networking in such contexts, I thought again how I should test my hypothesis. I would discover the extent to which he reproduced his earlier writing. This would provide a conclusive insight into his thought process, and the influence of his childhood, which was also my own childhood. That would allow me, in turn, to more clearly distinguish my thought from his thought. It would enable me to better identify the distance, the gulf, between us, which felt necessary given the extent to which he had in recent years imitated my own writing in tone and content. Given the extent to which he imitated my thought, used my vocabulary, and so on, it was inevitable that I would need to investigate him, I thought, and do so in this way, to re-establish the distance between us. I knew that I had escaped my formative imprisonment. Of that I was convinced. But there was still a chance that I had not entirely released myself from every aspect of it. There could be features of my thought and intellect that were not as original as I supposed, that extended into this century the false ideas and presuppositions of the last. Although I had demonstrably escaped my childhood and my childhood conditioning in a way that he had not, I could not be entirely sure that my escape was complete in every respect. This was precisely the reason why I needed to investigate the problem by inspecting his thought and his writing, a problem of such seriousness that it completely justified any discomfort I would cause him. He was, after all, already the victim of his childhood and his childhood conditioning. I merely wished to establish the extent of his victimhood. He was probably responsible for launching me on this investigation anyway, given what he once told me about his suspicions regarding himself, that he found himself using the same little phrases when addressing his children, and with the same intonation that his parents and grandparents had used with him. This led him, as he told me, to ask himself just how ancient those expressions and gestures were. He was led to question himself, as he once confessed, and wonder how much of himself was the repetition of gestures, phrases, and ticks, passed from one generation to the next. Most of these phrases were unrepeatable before another adult, he told me, but he did call his first son Old Chap, for instance, which is what his father called him as a boy, although his mother resented it, making him wonder how many generations of sons had been called Old Chap before him in that lineage, and how many mothers had resented it in turn. Or perhaps it came from a book. Perhaps that is where his father came across it, although even then it would be a memory and a trace, he decided, because books originate nothing. His mother, he said, preferred Little Man, which she would have never come up with, he mused, as I listened, if not for his father saying Old Chap, and he went on talking much along those lines as I wondered how, exactly, I was going to release myself from him this time, since everything he said bored me, and this more than ever. Another example, he said, was how he frowned whilst looking forward, his head tilted. He frowned at me looking right through his brows. My brows, he said, are heavy just like my father's. When I look through them, I look just like my father did when he looked at me. He repeated his mother's gestures too, he thought. When he raised his finger, curved slightly, and held it by the cheek, he looked just like his mother, he said. I look just like mother did when I hold my finger like this, he went on, holding his finger by his cheek. By that point I was beginning to boil a bit. He could not even hold his head in his hands, he went on, boring me with it still, without thinking of how she had held her own, he said. When he held his head in his hands he always thought of his mother. If he ever wanted to remember his mother, he would only have to hold his head in his hands. Whenever I think of mother, he said, I hold my head like that. He speculated that perhaps he repeated many other phrases and gestures unknowingly, but that is as far as he took it. Once I was finally free of him, and had begun to relax, I found myself thinking about what he had said, and, as I did so, took his thought about Old Chap and so on further than he ever did, and began to suspect that his entire frame of reference, his bearing, his speech, his habits, unthinkingly reproduced those he first encountered as a child. His childhood had the strongest impression on him as his small brain formed, trimmed back its neurones, and solidified, becoming the adult brain that now besieged me with his wonderings about the genealogy of expressions like Old Chap. Since my brain solidified at a similar time, or at least at a time not entirely unlike his own, we were only three years apart after all, and since our families had so much to do with one another and occupied the same context, in history, religion, climate, and so on, I did worry that my mind might also reflect our upbringing in thought and gesture in such a way that the diminished outlook I saw quite clearly in everything he thought and produced might also operate, concealed, behind my own intellectual production. This influence was, so I feared, far greater than the ordinary influence of childhood upon adulthood, given the extraordinary circumstances of our upbringing. He suffered his childhood and remained imprisoned by it more than any other person I have met, and to an extent even Freud would not admit possible, that is to say, his imprisonment took hold on an intellectual plane, not a subconscious one, not that I have any respect for Freud, or what Freud might think. But this would explain why his presence struck me so badly. With every irksome thing he said I could feel symptoms of my own imprisonment. This became my reason for resisting his thought and refusing his presence, a justification I developed to explain myself to myself, having done both, having resisted his thought, and having refused his presence, for as long as I could recall, intuitively, without knowing precisely, as I now knew, that it was necessary to resist, refuse, and diminish him for my own intellectual survival. I had the occasion to visit him some days later, and for a second time stole his entire life's work, as he called it. I stuffed the whole manuscript in my bag and avoided him for at least two weeks with complete success, though not without considerable effort, given that he must have been searching hard for his notes, and did come looking for me, hoping I might be of some help. By the time we met more than two weeks later, he had already stopped searching for his lost work, since, as he explained, every moment he occupied looking for his writing he might have better spent remembering it, and not forgetting it, as he feared. It was crucial, he argued, to cease searching and begin remembering as soon as the search itself seemed pointless. I held on to the papers for the next few months, not looking at them at all. It served no purpose to read the thing without a comparison set for which I would have to wait another year most likely, since he was busy producing it from memory a second time. The annual conference came round and yet again he gave his talk to the considerable disgruntlement but no longer shock of the other delegates who had already booked another room in preparation, and to which they slyly decanted. He gave a similar introduction in which he explained that he would, for another conference running, be unable to present original ideas since he had suffered the improbable loss, once more, of his entire life's work. He explained that although he had managed to reproduce much of that work, almost word for word in parts, he had been unable to reas- semble all the sources he had drawn upon, and quoted from, in order to compose the original argument, so that what he now offered, in this talk, was his argument on its own, without the supporting mate- rial, with no sources, references, and footnotes, and so on, to sub- stantiate its claims, even though he did assure us that the work he now gave an account of was based on the most careful and diligent scholarship, and that he would, in time, track down all the sources that supported his argument and insert them back where they belonged. He had not done so, not yet, having spent every moment available to him over the last few months remembering his argu- ment—a desperate, painful task, he told us—but now, given that this work was nearly complete, he would proceed to add the sources and back-fill, as he put it, the argument that he had already accomplished. Clearly for my experiment I would have to avail myself of this set of papers too, the most recent version of his so-called life's work, which I did, again stuffing the manuscript in my bag so that I now had in my possession two versions of that work ready for comparison. I knew this would repeat the cycle he had already been through for two years running, and that he would spend the next year painfully reassembling his thought, three times lost. This was inevitable. And necessary. As before I found some pretext to visit him, and when he was least suspecting took the latest set of papers from his brown leather case and stowed them in my bag, spending the next fortnight in a state of alertness should I need to flee if I saw him approaching. At work I placed the two stacks of paper on my desk, and regarded them when I remembered them, as I attended to a variety of urgent and pressing tasks, intending to look at the two sets as soon as I was able, and submit them to a thorough comparison so that I might judge just how diminished his outlook was, and discover which parts of his argument related most directly to his childhood experience, his experience which was his imprisonment, an experience that I also shared, in part, and to which I was at pains to ensure my thought bore no relation. If my thought did bare any relation to his I would be able, finally, to fully extract my thought from that prison life of our first years. I would make off with my thought, freshly liberated, and travel with it, going far beyond him and anything he could imagine or imitate, so that when I wrote and when I spoke nobody would make the mistake of associating the two of us. Several months later the papers still sat on my desk, now covered over by other papers from my professional responsibilities, since I had been too busy, really, to look at them and begin the extremely demanding and time-consuming task of the comparative work I had planned. Despite the personal importance of that work of comparative analysis—and when I say personal importance, I actually mean *vital importance*, because I am referring here to a project that is vitally important to me and everything I represent, a project that will be essential to the further development of my thought, and not only the denial of his non-thought—well then, it was important for me to begin the job, the immense analytic task, when I was in the right frame of mind, and was thereby ready for the kind of examination, which would also be an act of self-examination, that the task presented. Comparative analysis, I assured myself, would indeed reveal those passages that most reflected his childhood experience and the imprisonment of his mind, since it was impossible, I knew, that he could reproduce exact passages from memory. This was something I told myself repeatedly. Surely, I said to myself, any exact reproductions, or even similar passages, would reflect the unthinking operations of his unreflecting mind. These would be the most diminished, imprisoned thoughts he had ever produced. If these repeated passages resembled in any way anything I had independently thought, in content, or mood, or in some other respect, I would pursue those thoughts in my own work and intellect and be sure to be rid of them. I would reissue or redact any of my published works that had been infected. My writing would be suitably adjusted, and I would inspect each subsequent thought or intuition I had for traces of his thought, the mood of it, and so on. Comparative analysis would reveal precisely those commonalities between my thought and his, similarities that expressed the same narrow upbringing we suffered as children as we were introduced to a world that infected our minds and forever diminished our perspectives, confining us within the teachings of Christian Science alongside all the other narrow parochialisms that our culture brought us up on. This would be an excellent opportunity to interrogate my own thought by way of his non-thought and trim my thought down to its most original, revolutionary components. Once I had finished this task of comparative analysis my thought would be reduced to its revolutionary substrate. I would reissue my writing, I would rewrite the whole lot if necessary, and would produce work of such potency and venom, writing of such distinguished originality and force, that my thought would never be confused with his, but more than that, it would place my mind at the forefront, not simply at the forefront of my discipline, but at the forefront of my times, I would join the intellectual vanguard of my generation leaving the next few generations with the work of studying my own labours, labouring in the wake of that influence, catching up with what we achieved and understood years before they would achieve anything even remotely similar. Naturally they would produce their own originals, they would flay my language and turn it inside out, they would pile on imagery or cut it out and reverse assumptions and think themselves completely radical in their linguistic excess, or their linguistic poverty, but finally they would return to my writing, my writing expunged of his writing, and they would see that all they produced was already redundant, a mere froth, intellectual writerly foam, and would return to the measured but necessarily revolutionary radicalism of my own writing. Or the potency of my writing, or at least the solidity of my writing. They would return to my writing in any case, and regard it as solid, as a solid mass, even if it was not necessarily radical, even if it did not stand up and measure well against their own, they would recognise its solidity. They would look at it and say to themselves, *Well at least his writing was solid*. If nothing else his was a solid form of writing, and so on. They would see within my sentences what I went through to produce them, what I put him through in order to produce this writing. They would understand that even if I didn't kill him and only caused his death, the cost of his life was nothing to pay for the longevity of my writing. They would see that when it comes to writing of world-historical importance, or disciplinary significance, or merely, in my case perhaps, of personal significance, it is necessary to suspend moral restraints and overcome the social niceties, the good manners that tie us down otherwise. And they would understand that this can be achieved after all in a restrained but ruthlessly methodical manner, in a potent way, through writing that is solid, that lands itself in the ground and becomes lodged there and just sits there declaring itself. They would see that even solid writing and study can launch itself into a realm beyond moral restraint, not that I ventured far into that realm. Admittedly, with all I achieved in the realm of thought, with all my attempts to think beyond moral restraint, I still sat here at his wake looking at the ear, unable to move my chair because I was tied there by guilt, and politeness, and my fear that the son would look up and see me gone. My writing had really not taken me that far out of myself after all. This all testifies, I think, to the urgency of the task before me, the problem of comparative analysis, although by the occasion of the next conference a year later, I had not yet found the time for this essential task, given my other pressing commitments, and the need to find just exactly the right moment to begin—the task was, after all, immense—so that it came about that for the fourth year in succession he presented his paper from the floor, beginning by way of an introduction with an account of the unexpected loss, once again, of his life's work, which he had only coped with, he told us, due to the urgent necessity of reclaiming from his mind the thoughts that he had once had, which helped distract him from the pain of that oddly recurrent loss, three years running now, since every thought expended on the fact of that loss was a lost opportunity for reclaiming in writing what had once been written. This subsequent round of rewriting and reclaiming that he had embarked upon should not have been necessary, at least not for my purposes, since I had, as I initially thought, no need of a third copy, and had not wished him to produce it. He submitted himself to that torture on his own. I never asked him to do it, never suggested it to him, and certainly did not desire it. Naturally I might have returned at least one of those manuscripts in my possession by some anonymous chance, something untraceable to me, so as to alleviate his suffering, and yet for that to happen I needed to finish the task of comparative analysis that had lain before me on my desk for the last eleven months, and before that I had to begin, which might sound straightforward enough, but to begin requires the right moment. It should be obvious to anyone that anything worth doing cannot begin at any moment of time. It did nonetheless occur to me as I watched him in the foyer after his unwelcome presentation, standing with his coffee, as he sipped it, and as I sipped mine at a distance, regarding him with the brown leather case and the full set of pages from the last year's effort, that it would be interesting to look at that set as well, which was now the third complete iteration in existence—it would be the fourth if I had not destroyed the first stack— and compare the three of them together. This thought led me to again visit him at his house so that I might take his life's work, only he now kept it in a very definite place, he told me, somewhere hidden where it could not be disturbed or inadvertently mislaid, as if he no longer trusted himself not to misplace it. I would have to employ all my ingenuity here, not to locate the papers, which was after all not that difficult, but to get their location from him in a manner that would not generate suspicion when they subsequently disappeared. He was still remarkably unsuspecting given that for three years running his life's work had gone missing shortly after I visited, and it had never occurred to him, so far as I could tell, to wonder if I had some part in it. To get this latest version from him I was forced, despite myself, to ask him about his thought, and about his writing, so that he would be encouraged to go and get his papers. I had to ask him to read to me the relevant passage that might answer my question, my question-as-pretext, which happened to be about the medieval mind, and thereby show me where his papers were now kept. It turned out that the papers were very close to hand indeed, stuffed right under the seat on which I sat, a leather armchair on which I had been waiting wondering about their whereabouts and from which he extracted his notes in order to tell me what, precisely, he had devised regarding my question relating to his work on *the medieval mind*. I had to stand up as he knelt down to extract the papers that were tightly wedged under the armchair and were dog-eared from his evident stuffing under and retrieving from that place, a process he must have repeated each time he set to work on the next stage of his writing, or rewriting to put it more precisely, which was in his case a form of non-writing. To avoid raising suspicion I feigned continued interest, and again, despite myself, let myself in for a long evening of discussion regarding his views on the matter relating to *the medieval mind*, prompted by my reluctantly asked question, which tended more in the direction of a monologue as I sat, and he read his notes, occasionally embellishing but largely reading the stuff so that in actual fact his presence was hardly required. I might just as well have read them on my own, I thought, although I would never have read them, of course, but would have put them down at the earliest opportunity given that they were useless to me on their own without the other two versions placed alongside. These notes were only interesting to me from the perspective of the comparative study that I anticipated, they held no interest in themselves and were painful to listen to given that I had no desire to hear what he thought, for its own sake, since his thought had no broader significance beyond relating certain childhood experiences that he had not escaped, and that I shared, and which really I did not need to know any more about than I already did, even in the sublimated form of his writing, as it imitated mine, and plagiarised my interests. The problem of extracting it from him, of stealing his so-called life's work at its last iteration, occupied me as he spoke, since presumably only I, in addition to him, knew where his notes were now kept, and so if they did indeed vanish, as planned, he would surely suspect me, although I felt that he trusted me still, as though it had not yet occurred to him that my orientation towards him was strained, if not profoundly coloured by negative feeling. There was no way I could make off with his life's work under these conditions without arousing suspicion, and this placed me in an awkward position as I sat, listening to him talk, suffering his ideas, as he looked at me with that desperate look he had when he looked at me, given how urgently he wished to be heard. He told me that he intended to tell the story of education in the language of sickness, and that, in response to my question, this accounting, his accounting for *the medieval mind* in its relation to the problem of sickness, was a key stage in his analysis. I nodded, as he looked at me, urgently, as if he needed me to receive his ideas, and nod at them, for them to properly exist. My listening to him was clearly a crucial stage in the development or at least affirmation of his thought, a step that might finally confirm the great significance of the ideas he had been working on, that he had been rewriting for a third time these last few months. Exploring *the medieval mind* in its relation to the problem of sickness, he confirmed, was absolutely essential to telling the story of education in the language of sickness. I looked at him and wondered again about the problem of extracting these notes, now on his lap, and which he presently held, without him realising it was me. If he realised, or even just suspected I took them, I would have no rest from his questioning. He would seek me out tirelessly, wishing to somehow rescue his so-called life's work so that he might finish it, make something of it, and then, presumably, eventually prepare it for final publication, although no one would touch his work, I knew, given that he commanded no respect and no publisher would consider the work of an author, a completely unknown author, with nobody to vouch for his intellect. This, or something like it, is what I was thinking as he said to me, with that desperate look, *We cannot understand the story of education told in the language of sickness*. He paused, I think expecting me to nod again, which I refused to do. We cannot understand education in the language of sickness, he continued, because education in the modern understanding is synonymous with health, even though education in my understanding, he went on, is actually synonymous with sickness. The problem with the idea of education, he said, is its assumed positivity. Education is a positive word, he told me, as I looked back, blankly. This was probably one of the most banal things he had ever said, I thought. Education is basically a synonym for health, he added, needlessly. Hence, we cannot understand the story of education told in the language of sickness, he said, returning to his first point, because education is basically a synonym for health, he reiterated, turning to his second point. I wondered how long this would continue. It is for this reason, he went on, that we must contrast medieval conceptions of what I call *education as sickness*, with modern conceptions of education and health. We must do this, he said, in order to understand that education does not necessarily have to be associated with healthiness, as if education were basically a synonym for health, where to become educated, he went on, is to be improved, bettered, enhanced as a being, and not rendered by way of education more sick, which is the hypothesis I have been testing in these pages that are my life's work, he added, and which I have spent the last few months rewriting from memory once again as you know. I noted that when he said, *as you know*, he said these words entirely without emphasis. The words *as you know* were delivered perfectly flat. This reassured me. When we think of education we think of improvement, he repeated, and health, not ill-health and sickness. It is my life's work, he went on, to set out what we are determined not to see, not as educated beings at least, and this is the hypothesis, my hypothesis, he said, that education and sickness have long been, *and remain*, he emphasised, co-implicated. Education and sickness are not simply related, he continued, they are not cousins, they are combined together. That, he said, is the hypothesis I have been pursuing, the idea I have been working through in my head, an idea, an entire landscape in thought that nobody else will see until I finally show it to them. Education and sickness function together, he said, labouring the point somewhat. To become educated is to become sick. *That is my basic hypothesis*, he repeated as I sat in the leather chair wondering how long this would last. I should apologise, he said to me, for not having all the necessary sources at my disposal, all the source material that I once consulted which would back up all the claims I make in these papers, he told me, patting the stack of papers on his lap, though I will, with time, he went on, ensure that I find those sources again and back-fill, as he called it, my argument, so that it can again rest in the evidence from which it was once written. But the lack of evidence, he continued, as I sat, is not what holds my argument back, since my audience, which is all educated people after all, will struggle to appreciate my argument, not for lack of supporting evidence but due to the fact that for today's educated person it is unthinkable that education and sickness might be intimately related. I can say *to become educated is to become sick* as much as I like, he said, but they will never hear it. It is unthinkable, this claim, my claim, that to become a bit more educated is always, in effect, to become a bit more sick. Hence the need, he added, as I sat, for a stark historical contrast. I will jolt the educated with my stark historical contrast, he went on. My stark historical contrast will enable the educated to finally see how *to become educated is to become sick.* I will present them with my stark historical contrast in an account, in a truly audacious, a fully justified account, he added, of the very different cosmology that framed the outlook of the medieval mind. For the medieval mind, he said, education and sickness were not opposed but were combined, as will be indicated in the conceptual term I have just introduced, namely, the idea of *education as sickness*, which I may well hyphenate as *education-as-sickness*, he said, hyphenating the words with his hands to really nail the point home. He emphasised the term with his hands held out like that as I sat listening, sitting in the armchair, knowing as I did what I needed to know about the location of his so-called life's work, that was, as chance had it, stowed under the very chair I had chosen to sit on before asking him, with my ulterior motive, about *the medieval mind*, a term that I had no respect for, but that I knew preoccupied him, and so would perform the task well enough of prompting him to reveal the location of his papers, quite unsuspectingly, as I hoped. He would be so enthralled that I finally wished to hear his thought on *the medieval mind* that he would never suspect me and realise that my intention was not, after all, to hear about *the medieval mind*, but to make off again with his life's work. I could see now at the wake, as I looked at the copy on my lap, at the final copy of his life's work, at his final manuscript, or the death manuscript as I have decided to call it, that the phrase *education-as-sickness* was probably underlined, or given some kind of emphasis on the page he read to me more than a year before, since I had finally reached the respective page in the pile on my lap where the phrase was indeed emphasised like that on the next iteration that he had rewritten from memory, the fifth iteration of his life's work, the last iteration he produced before he died. His son was still in that indeterminate state, somewhere between wakefulness and sleep, or so it looked, so that I, desiring not to look at the corpse, but equally unable to get up and move about, perhaps to go to the kitchen for a drink, found myself looking further through the pages in that typewritten manuscript, really just a collection of notes. It had clearly been dropped at least once and reassembled so that parts were completely disordered, although others were clipped together, such as these notes that I now looked at, recalling in my mind that evening over a year ago when I endured the fourth iteration of his life's work only so I could subsequently make off with it for the purposes of my comparative analysis. I would like to suggest, he said, as I sat in the armchair, there has been a significant shift in relation to the question of sickness, between the medieval period, and the period of modern education. This, he went on, is the nub of my stark historical contrast, this shift, he said, and as I now read in the death manuscript, which might be useful in shedding some light on what is unique about our period, and about how it understands the project of education. I have picked a comparatively distant period, he went on, because I think it provides a useful contrast, a stark contrast, a necessary contrast. The medieval period, he continued, presents an educational system that is sufficiently alien for us to see what is distinct about our own educational order. In the medieval context sickness was directly educational. In the modern context, sickness and education part ways. In the medieval context, he repeated, education and sickness are associates, in the modern context they are presumed opposed. As he spoke, the exact plan for stealing his life's work a fourth time formulated in my mind. I decided that he must not be allowed to return the pages of his life's work to its original position under the seat on which I was sitting. There was no question of him returning his life's work to that particular hiding place, which is what prompted me to remark, off-handedly, *It smells damp*, and ask if he could detect the smell too. Can you smell it, I said, to which he replied, No he could not, and then continued with, *So why do I persist* with this hypothesis of mine about sickness, if sickness and education are now considered opposed, and if the entire premise of modern education is based on that opposition. Well, he said, despite the fact that education and sickness are now considered antithetical, or mutually incompatible, so that it has become almost unthinkable to align education with sickness or to speak of education in terms of sickness or in the language of sickness, I would like to suggest, he said, that sickness *still performs* an important if disavowed function in modern education. This function is difficult to perceive or understand, he explained, because of the alignment between education and health, namely, the fundamental idea that good education is intrinsically healthy in the broad, social, political, and moral sense of that word. We are entirely ruled by this idea, he went on, that education is the basis of health, that education is necessary for the health of the individual and the health of society. Which is why I needed a stark historical contrast in order to disturb that idea, even though it rules us, and will not be disturbed, I suspect, he said, at least not without considerable difficulty, he added, and perseverance, if not a little genius, he said, looking at me as I stared back blankly. *Are you sure*, I asked him, *that you cannot smell it too*, to which he replied again that he could not, and returning to his notes, continued with his reading, perhaps a little doubtful by now that I was properly attending to his argument. *Education and sickness are still treated as separate entities*, with medicine taking care of the latter, *as you know*, he said. This time there was emphasis. *As a profoundly sick person you know that*, he added, trying to personalise things and somehow secure my interest. I did hate it when he personalised things. It was a technique he adopted when he saw my attention drift. He would see my attention drift and then dredge up something from our mutual experience, something from our past, in order to return my attention to his point. I called it his biographical opportunism. He would come at me with his biographical opportunism and remind me of experiences we had once shared for the sole purpose of returning me to his argument. His biographical opportunism had no other function, I thought, than that, excepting the other purpose of reminding me just how much common experience we had, making the point all too deliberately, I thought, that we were intimately connected when it came to our biographies. *You know well enough*, he said, about this arbitrary separation between education on the one hand and sickness on the other. Education and sickness are considered antithetical, but *you know* this is a contrived opposition. *You have experienced it*, he said to me, you have had direct experience of that false separation, as I recall well, he said. You have been in and out of hospital, he said to me, in and out of hospital, he repeated, and all your university employer managed by way of an allowance, he continued, was to give you some time off, your sick leave, but nothing much else. *Your university*, he said to me, got rid of you by having you sign yourself off sick. If you were sick enough, and could prove you were sick enough, you were not to work. You had to beg for it of course, he said, and really show that you were desperately sick, but once you did that, they washed their hands of you and told you to stay away. When you were sick enough, your educational employer told you to stay out of range, because it had no way of accommodating you in your sickness. They told you not to come back unless you were well enough to work. For your employer it was clear that if you returned to your desk for somewhere different to sit, if you visited your colleagues in their offices for a bit of company, or just went to your faculty grounds for a stroll, you could not be sick enough to be off sick and should return to work. They fulfilled their legal obligations to you, they paid your sick pay and told you to not return until you were able to stand without feeling queasy, until your doctor gave you a note to the effect that you were fit enough to come back. You could only return when you were no longer demonstrably sick enough to be at home. And when you came back you were still a liability, he reminded me. You would still faint at inconvenient moments, or if not faint, you would still need to take a seat at times because it was too much for you to stand, and finally, he said, do you remember that day, I remember it, he said, when you stared at me with horror, do you recall, he said, that day you stared like that, the day your eyes nearly popped out of your head from fear and desperation, as I told you after, the day I came along the corridor and you started twisting about on the floor, confronting your colleagues with the prospect of a death in the building as you held your chest and feared for your end, and you looked at me, do you remember, he said, asking me to help you as you lay there on the floor in so much pain, because I remember it, he said, I remember it very well, I have not forgotten the sight of you dropping to the floor, looking at me in desperation, fearing you would die with your eyes nearly popping out of your head, as I told you after, because the way your eyes looked was really odd, he went on, and I thought you should be aware just how odd you looked on the floor, looking at me, begging me to help and not let you die. I had no idea what to do, he said. I looked at you and knew that I had no idea what to do with you, but do you remember what I said, he asked me, do you remember the words I used as you lay there, he said, the words I soothed you with as you looked at me with your eyes very nearly popping out of your head, because I recall them, he went on, I remember exactly what I said, I used those words our parents used with us when we were children, those words they used when we fell and cried and they said these things to soothe us, helping us with their words because sickness for them, as you know, was supposed to be an illusion. As you lay there I used those same words to soothe you, even though you and I no longer believe in them, and do you remember what happened, do you remember it, he said, they worked after all, because your eyes stopped popping and you started to breathe again, even though we no longer believe in those words, they worked for you then, he said, which is the strangest thing, he told me, us not believing in the words but the words still working, because they soothed you, I could see that, as I said these words without thinking, they helped you when you felt that was it. *This is it*, as you said, saying those words with a touch of melodrama as it turned out, he added. When you said that, when you gasped those words, you said them needlessly as it happened. When you said those words, I was there by your side, listening carefully. I clearly remember you saying, *This is it*, and we all heard you say it, I have to say, we heard you very well between your gasps, we all heard you say that, and I am sure your colleagues still remember it, and probably still talk about it, because I remember hoping as I heard you say those words that you were exaggerating and being melodramatic, which in the end you were. *This is it* was a melodramatic thing for you to say, as it turned out. It was an extraordinary bit of melodrama for you to say that. True, you were very ill, your illness was severe, but it added a touch of melodrama to the occasion for you to say that, as it happened. And then, after all that, after that serious yet by no means deadly event, you returned to work. Do you remember, he asked me needlessly, you were back at work a few weeks later with the same colleagues who could still remember how odd you looked, how strange your expression was, and how your eyes were, as you lay there. You were at work again with the exact same people who saw you lie in my arms and look at me and say, *This is it*, even though that was not it, and you would not die after all, and you saying *This is it*, was, if nothing else, factually incorrect. Following your operation and those weeks in hospital you eventually returned, I remember it, you were still profoundly ill, but you returned. And even then it was presumed that your return to work in the educational establishment that employs you *was a sign of health*, he said, *do you remember*, he added needlessly. The more your workplace loads you with work, the more recovered you are presumed to be, he said. When your workload was back to its usual level and you were entirely loaded up and you bore it all, when you carried your workload at its full capacity, exactly *that* was taken as a sign of health. He is fully recovered, your colleagues thought. After all that, he is fully recovered. Look, he is better. When you could stand again and deliver your lectures without needing to sit because you thought you would faint, this was taken to be a further sign of recovery. But I know, and you know, that you never recovered and will be in and out of hospital again. Your recovery, he said, was a false recovery, and you will be back in hospital before you know it. Your condition is a terminal condition, he reminded me, and there is no escaping it. One day you will be right to say *This is it*, and you might not have to wait all that long to do so. I remember, he said, that even when you were in hospital and your doctors observed that you were, again, able to read, able to hold a book, they assumed it was a sign of recovery. You were after all returning to a higher state of health, they thought, I suspect, than the one in the bed opposite, do you remember, the illiterate one, the one with no teeth, who, by comparison to you, a highly educated man, could only return to a different state of health, a lower state of health, a form of animal health, if that isn't putting it too crudely, he added, and looked, and I looked back giving nothing away, and so he began to wonder, I thought, or appear to wonder if this had taken it too far. I only speak here on behalf of the principles I am criticising, he then added, as if that saved his argument. I parody those principles, he said. I place those principles within my sentences only to parody them, he assured me. Because on behalf of the principles I am criticising, he went on, the man opposite was an uneducated man, a toothless man, and could only return to a lower state of health. This is not my view, he said, but from the perspective of the principles that I am criticising, the man before you, on the other bed, was worth less than you, he was clearly worth less than you, the educated man, even if nobody will ever say that out loud, the principles themselves are clear enough, the evaluative order, he said, the moral frame we live within is clear enough about the fact that the man in the other bed was less than you and could only return to a lower state of health. The presumptions here are all wrong, of course, he said, but that is how they stand. All of this must be overthrown, he told me, but that is how things are. *You have seen it*, he said, you have experienced it. You know better than anyone else that what I say is true. As I hated him personalising his argument, I did not acknowledge it. I think I did not react at all to all this. I sat in the armchair completely impassive. I wished merely to wait it out, to endure it until finally he stopped speaking and I could leave. I was only listening to him talk so long, and was only enduring his perspective in this way, because it was essential he did not suspect me of asking him about *the medieval mind* as a mere pretext to stealing his manuscript. I could not fail to recall his hospital visits when I lay incapacitated having no way of escape, and felt now, as I felt then, that his ability to visit me in the ward, and my inability to escape, was the worst part of my stay in that hospital, worse than everything else they did to me there, which was bad in itself, as I was prodded and treated with abstract suspicion. The doctors viewed me as a suspicious object. I could tell they saw me like that, however much they, too, attempted to personalise things and make light of my morbid condition, a condition they still had no name for. They kept referring to it as *your condition*, by which they meant my morbid condition, or sometimes to *your attack*, but these words merely covered up the fact that they had absolutely no idea what precisely was wrong with me. They treated me without knowing what was wrong with me, and I had the feeling that the doctors who saw me were only waiting for my condition to improve, or for it to worsen. They were simply waiting for my condition to change. They were spectators, I felt, rather than actors. With this one, they decided, they had no agency and so they merely spectated. My doctors had no idea what was wrong with me, so they watched me instead. They wondered if he would get better or if he would get worse, and they came each day to find out which it was. Meanwhile, he kept visiting me in hospital, and stayed for hours by contrast to the doctors who came for minutes, if that. They popped in, satisfied their curiosity, and walked out, whereas he took a chair and sat there for much of the day, talking to me as I lay trapped, telling me about what he was thinking, and then, occasionally, recalling the events of *your attack*. He heard the doctors call it that. *Do you remember*, he would say each time before describing the events. *Do you remember*, he repeated, before telling me how I looked, and then recalling exactly what he did in response. I lay trapped in in that hospital as he said, *Do you remember*, and suffered his recollections. Months later, as I sat in the armchair, sitting there, in the armchair, thinking about the manuscript that I would steal, I could not fail to remember how it felt to lie in that hospital bed unable to escape his visits. In the period we call modernity, he went on, as I sat in the armchair, education and medicine are separate domains. They only involve themselves with one another under certain conditions, he added. Modern medicine will involve itself in educational settings only to make them *healthier*, through the inoculation of schoolchildren, or recommendations regarding school hygiene, for instance. Medicine, he said, does not intervene in order to make those settings more *educational*. Medicine and education are, at this level, clearly distinguished in their aims. I was hardly listening. Critical educational thought, he continued, is underpinned by the belief that when medical words and medical concepts stray beyond the domain of responsibility given over to clinical medicine, they have gone too far. This must be resisted as the medicalization of educational space. The same goes for psychology, which I consider a branch of medicine, he said. When education is reconceptualised as *therapy*, as so-called circle time, or whatever, this again must be resisted as the undue psychologization of educational space. The purity of educational space must be protected, these educationalists claim, from intrusion, they say. And yet by contrast, the reverse process, the *educationalization* of medicine, or the *educationalization* of psychology, are never presented as matters of concern, since education is a universal idea. The reach of education, for us moderns, has to extend everywhere. It is possible to intrude on education, to distort it, to debase its mission, but not the opposite given that there is no limit to the reach of education. Yet education does intrude on all other domains, he went on, even if nobody notices, he added, and it does so with such ease because each intrusion is understood as a sign of educational advancement. By this point I had almost given up listening. The intrusion of education, he went on, the intrusion of education to all domains, the *educationalization* of something, of all things, of everything, can only be understood as an improvement in the condition of things, he said, at least that is how it looks from the modern perspective, *our perspective*, he added with emphasis. The educationalization of all domains can only be understood as the situation of their improvement, he repeated. To make something educational is always to make it better, which is why, although nobody will admit it, he added, you as the educated man were superior to the toothless man in your ward, even when you were very ill, even when you were, in a medical sense, far worse off than he was. That man could only be improved to the extent that he was educated, he said. This is the brutal truth of education, he said to me, this is the basic assumption that underpins the self-understanding of all educated people, he added. Medicine can heal, but only education can improve. Because you did not teach him, he told me, that man was not improved, he was only healed. Because you only read your books to yourself, you left him in his animal health, he went on, or his near-animal health, he clarified, looking at me for some kind of reaction. You maintained the separation between the work of education and the work of medicine, he told me, by leaving that man unattended, by failing to improve him, you did that, he said. Despite your intellect and those weeks you spent in the presence of that man, you did not talk to him, you did not listen to him, you left him in his condition, a situation where he was only attended by medical professionals, and never by educational professionals. The latter had long abandoned him. His teachers abandoned him when he was still a boy. You arrived on his ward and then you did it too. But you did not see it that way, of course. You maintained the division between the work of your educational establishment and the work of the hospital because that is a natural division and it should never have occurred to you to sit up and give the man a lesson, even if he could receive it, which most likely he could not, because he was not just illiterate and toothless, but old. The illiterate man, the toothless man, was old, and so it was too late for him. There are exceptions, he said, like teaching hospitals, but teaching hospitals do not teach their patients to read, they only teach their staff how to administer medical care. So exceptions exist, he admitted. As you will tell me, there are always exceptions, he told me, but you were not one of them. So yes, exceptions do exist, and yet even if it is admitted that education is in league with medicine to some extent, he said, and not only in the teaching hospital but across the board, it becomes only harder to confront the more basic possibility that *education is in league with sickness*. He left a pause at that point, which was some relief, even if the space he left was filled with expectation, since he clearly felt that his argument had reached some kind of peak. I am definitely sure I smell damp, I concluded. He did not reply, and said, perhaps not word for word, *I would still argue, though*, that modern education is borne of an engagement with sickness and exists in relation to it. That is my hypothesis, he repeated, and slapped himself on the thigh. Education is riveted on sickness though it will not declare or admit that dependence. He slapped himself again. Education is haunted by sickness but would prefer to proceed as if it had nothing to do with the sickness it produces and depends upon. Another slap. Even as you lay there in hospital after *your attack*, he said, education was still making you sick, he told me. When your doctors saw that you had the strength again to raise a book and read it, they took that as a sign of your recovery. Look, he is on the up, they said when they next checked in on you. But this reading you were doing was only making you sick again, he said. The whole idea that your reading was making you sick, that your recovery was a false recovery, and that it was so precisely because you were reading, is an idea that nobody will understand, he told me. Nobody will understand that statement because it is an impossible statement to understand. The educated cannot understand the notion that education was, at that point in your recovery, still making you sick, as you lay there with the strength now to read, and that it worked harder to make you sick the more you recovered and the more you were able again to read. This is an impossible statement, he said, my claim is beyond the comprehension of educated people, he went on, because education is a positive idea and the educated are formed to understand education as a positive idea, even if they are surrounded by negativity, even if everything that is educated and that stands about them presents a landscape of pure negativity, the educated will still believe that education is basically a positive notion. Consequently, all educational activities are positive activities, at least in their intent, or in their potential. They are opposed to sickness, to ill-health, to darkness. But the insistent positivity of modern education, he went on, is only the product of this reaction against sickness, he said, which is itself a form of sickness, he added. The relentlessly positive attitudes of those who speak on behalf of education, on behalf of its institutions, its cultural achievements, can be taken as a sign of that denial, of a defence of education and educated culture that is haunted by the sickness it creates. Defenders of education and educated culture are entirely demented, I recall him saying, they are determined to see every negative aspect of education as an example of corruption, rather than as a manifestation of the truth of education in its corrupted, inherently diseased, and sick-making condition. They cannot see the disease that is built into education, that is integral to it, driven as they are to maintain their ideal of education in all its bleached positivity. At this point in his monologue, or somewhere thereabouts, I lowered myself from the leather armchair to the carpet and, bending over, began to smell the floor, eventually tilting the armchair a little with one hand so that I might press the carpet underneath with the other and say, *I definitely smell damp*, and then look up, not at him, but at the papers on his lap. As I looked at the papers, the manuscript, his life's work, I considered saying, *Do you mind if I*, following which I would lean forward and place my nose by the papers and frown, saying nothing more, I should not overdo it. But then I decided that I had already done enough, and so returned to my chair with a *Do go on*, assured in my mind that enough had been done, perhaps a little too obviously, to convince him that there was, in this room, a definite case of rising damp, which is not at all unusual in houses of this age, and which does not constitute a problem, as such, although it is important in cases like these to make sure that the room in question is properly aired, that furniture is not pressed against the wall, and that there is enough air circulation around and below furniture to avoid the setting in of damp and the build-up of mildew. On reflection I am not quite sure if I did actually kneel on the carpet, I surely considered it, but perhaps only that, deciding instead that stating, *It smells damp*, was enough. He went on, but as he did so I was sure that as he read he was also thinking about my remark about the damp, so that he was just as preoccupied with the thought of damp as he was with the telling of his life's work, or that part of it which related to the question I had asked about *the medieval mind*. In its relation to sickness, he said, modern education carries forth more than a mere trace of its medieval ancestry, even though that connection is no longer explicitly acknowledged, of course. In a medieval context, sickness and divine instruction were intimate and prominently displayed, where the visibility of sickness ensured the purchase of divine instruction on the soul of the instructed. Medieval sickness was not owned by medicine, but by God, who, in His wisdom, would use sickness to teach the priesthood and its laity. The occasion of disease was as much a theological concern as it was a matter for medical doctors, he told me, so that when sickness was treated by medicine, it was understood within a frame of reference that was not yet divorced from theology. *To the medieval mind*, he said, with emphasis, as if to recall me to my question, the body manifested the lesson it both demanded and deserved. It was the means by which the soul was inspected. Upon its surface, each body could display the sign of a diseased self, where sickness was the outer manifestation of inner corruption. But the imprint of sickness was also the form that divine instruction took as it was wrought upon the body. Sickness *was* education, he said. Although God's instruction was violent, that violence made sense, *to the medieval mind*, he added. To the modern mind it makes no sense at all that education should be violent. To the modern mind violence represents a perversion of educational intent. To suggest that modern education involves some kind of violence will only be understood, *from the modern perspective*, he said, as an objection to a specific case of educational perversion, and as a demand to make education less violent and thereby bring out the essential non-violence of a perfected educational setting. This is an extremely odd presumption, he said, *from the medieval perspective*, he added. From the medieval perspective, he went on, education had to be violent. The imprint it left was not simply an indicator of God's wrath, of the eternal damnation that awaits all those who do not heed its warning signs. The violence of education was also a sign of divine mercy, where each violent mark bore the potential to instruct the sufferer in self-betterment. *Violence was necessary for moral improvement*, he told me, thinking, I suspect, that this last statement in particular would impress me. Here he allowed himself a diversion, suggesting to me that Kafka was basically medieval in his thought and writing, at least in his conception of punishment and education as it appears in the penal colony, you know, he said, the story, the short story, you know the one, the one he calls *In the Penal Colony*. As you must surely know, he went on, in that penal colony the death sentence is carved into the back of the condemned prisoner, he reminded me, as if I needed reminding. He quoted a line from memory, *You've seen that it's not easy to figure out the inscription with your eyes, but our man deciphers it with his wounds.* But this is by the by, he said, and I should not be diverted even though it would be a very interesting hypothesis to pursue, he said, that is, the extent to which Kafka dredged up medieval residues in this work, and in other writings too, so that Kafka was, in certain respects, a medieval thinker, or, to put it less strongly, so that Kafka did in some degree reflect a medieval perspective in his thought. He returned to his notes, and continued, *In its basic conception, medieval education acknowledged the necessity of violence, the necessary association of instruction and pain. In their teachings medieval educators openly considered the integral function of violence as they worked in the shadow of a vengeful God of discomfort, guilt, and atonement. Education, sickness, and violence were necessary associates*, he concluded. As I read all this in the death manuscript, I wondered how much of it was pure repetition of the second, third, and fourth iterations of his life's work. But I could only wonder at that, and could not judge, since I had not arrived at the wake prepared for the task of comparative analysis. I had no idea that I would be presented with the fifth iteration, the death manuscript, and would subsequently offer to spend the night with the body, and the son. At best I would be sitting here with Thomas Bernhard's

Extinction. But my daughter made that impossible. By the fourth iteration—the third full version of his life's work that I had preserved—
the task of comparative analysis had become much greater, and
hence, more off-putting, although it would also be more fruitful if I
ever got to it, helping triangulate and pinpoint exactly where his
thought repeated itself more or less perfectly, and so expressed most
definitely the effects of his childhood imprisonment. With the fifth
and final iteration now on my lap, the task of comparative analysis
was even more off-putting. With this version the task had grown in
scale once again. Nonetheless, any matched text would assuredly
show, more definitely than ever, that his capacity to reproduce his
thought word for word was indeed the sign of its production as a
reflex arc, as an extension of the effects of our common childhood
and his imprisonment. He wrote this fifth iteration, the one at the
wake, because I had of course managed to launch him on his fourth,
and what would turn out to be his final year of rewriting from memory.
The suggestion of damp did indeed cause him to store his life's work
in the old manner, this was over a year ago, as he placed it once more
on his desk in the brown leather case, on which the papers would not
be susceptible to mildew, and become rank, so that in a few days I
could make off with them without much suspicion. This would cause
him to repeat the cycle of reformulating his thought, urgently getting
it down on paper before he forgot it, though I would again make sure
that I spent at least two weeks avoiding him, just in case he burdened
me with his pain that yet again the unthinkable had happened and he
had lost his life's work. I sat in my office with the three iterations of
his life's work on my desk. My door was closed just in case he arrived,
and locked, so that if he did, I would not answer, and he would not
push it open. I had some urgent matters to attend to, and made my
way through a list of tasks, a list in the mind that forms in the office
as I complete one job, and remember several others, so that the list
grows with each completed job, and expands in such a way that by the
end of the morning I have no real idea what I have achieved. Even
though I can say that I have spent a good part of the morning, if not
most of it, doing something in a state of great busyness, I have the
strongest impression that I have more to do at the end of it than when
I started. It is not always like this. I am still capable of *not* forming

mental lists, which is what I do when I come to the office to think, but for thinking my mind must be at rest, or in a state of relaxation, and cannot, for instance, be dwelling on the possibility of interruption, which is what I was thinking about that morning when going through my list. Some way through the morning a man appeared at the end of a ladder—I could not see the bottom of it—to fix a downpipe on the building opposite. He had a tool of some sort in one hand, and a section of replacement downpipe in the other, which, after some amount of preparation, he attempted to put in position. The ladder was below the point to which the downpipe was to be fixed, an arrangement that had been perfectly necessary up until this moment, since the opening to the gutter, and the fixtures, had to be first readied. But once that was done, and it was time to insert the down-pipe, his ladder was clearly in the way, so that the ladder was no longer in a good position but was now in the worst possible position for completing the task. He did not descend to reposition the ladder, I noticed, but shuffled the top of it on which he stood to the left, jumping the top of the ladder out from the wall and over to the left so that the ladder was now slanted and would allow the downpipe to be positioned in place where the ladder had rested. As he finished the connection of the downpipe to the bottom of the gutter, now possible because the ladder had been moved and stood aslant, I had the feeling that at any moment his ladder would slip, which prompted a small sensation, fear for his safety but mainly a feeling of reluctance given that I would have to make the effort to unlock my office door, go down the stairs, and face the inevitable commotion. The man on the ladder did not in the end fall off, but the feeling of reluctance stayed with me and became a sense of guilt, or a sensation like it, which I then con-nected to the three manuscripts, and the accompanying fear that their author would come looking for them. This fear is what made me cold to the fate of a man who was, as far as I believed, about to be seriously injured in direct view of my desk. Unwilling to spend a fort-night at work worrying that he might approach, and that I might have to flee, I took two week's leave, leaving my daughter a note—she did worry about me—ending up after my journey at a small cottage on an island. It was carefully chosen so that I was completely unreachable with no forwarding address or other means by which I might be contacted. It was probably an over-reaction on my part. Perhaps I only wished for solitude and used him as my excuse. The effort of retrieving his ideas from the recesses of his mind, even if those ideas were in large part the reflexes of his childhood imprisonment, had taken its toll over the last year. He was notably thinner, and as his son later told me, struggled to eat even when food was delivered straight to his desk, since he was worried, as he ate, that he might forget something he needed to remember, a vital connection in his argument, that would be necessary if his life's work was to have the kind of persuasive force and deliver the kind of impact he felt it deserved. As the fifth iteration bore out, he had managed to reconstruct some fairly lengthy arguments, an achievement I could not help recognise, but he had plenty of practice by now. By this point he must have become pretty good at sitting down after the first fortnight of desperation, making himself calm so that he could begin the task of remembering the whole thing, paragraph by paragraph, line by line. He had to shut out his lamentations, overcome the feeling of loss and the need to mourn over all the mislaid work, the hours he would never get back, all the pain it had taken him to reproduce the whole thing yet again. He sat as previously and set to work, refusing food, even more ruthless to himself than before, utterly dedicated to the ordeal before him, shutting out the world for the last months of his life so that he would not be distracted by anything except the task of remembering all the lines and words of his life's work. I thought that his argument probably did alter over time, as only comparative analysis would demonstrate, drifting gradually from the ideas found in the second iteration, to the ideas found in the last, the death manuscript. As I sat facing his body, the ear, and the son, I worked my way further down the pile of pages on my lap, coming across another collection of papers clipped together at the corner, at least the first page of which was missing, so that it began, mid-sentence, with the words, *an act of divine, genocidal instruction that has to be the most violent representation of educational possibility in the medieval canon.* Stunning as this educational limit point may be, it went on, in the medieval economy of pain and discomfort lessons were mostly wrought and understood through cases of individual sickness rather than collective plague or disaster. I should clarify, he wrote, that I am addressing the period before the Black Death, or the Great Plague, of 1350, or thereabouts, which changed things, of course, given the extraordinary suffering it unleashed and all it wiped out, the millions of lives, and so on, which had repercussions, undoubtedly, for education of course, and the place of sickness in education too, he added, although I was really concerned with the period *before* the great pestilence. I was mostly preoccupied with various collections of Latin and vernacular *exempla*, he wrote, especially those on the topic of sickness. I remember him doing that reading, I thought, a good few years ago now it was. He went on and on at the time about these collections of *exempla* that he was working his way through and that I, at the time, had no interest in hearing about. They came to popular usage, he wrote, following the Fourth Lateran Council which met in 1215 or thereabouts to consider the declining quality of the priesthood, its general neglect of the laity, and more broadly, the spread of heresy. These short didactic texts were appended to the end of medieval church sermons and were, with time, gathered up in compendia that the priest might consult, rather like a dictionary of phrases, to say something that was both edifying and striking, and so wake up a congregation he had otherwise put to sleep. They targeted the unlearned Christian who did not understand Latin, who might benefit from something, a few words, that made at least some kind of sense, a story that would address them finally in the vernacular and deliver the lesson that the priest had decided upon that day. It struck me, he wrote, how often the exact malady, the precise sickness, remained unspecified. It was odd, I thought, he wrote, how sickness was invoked in these *exempla* without the story in question actually stating it—what it looked like, if it oozed how it oozed with puss and wherefrom it oozed, and so on—as if it hardly mattered, since it was not the point of the story to specify details like that. Each sickness functioned more often than not as a broad category, signifying a range of transgressions, and would, as such, take form in the story as an inexact malady standing for an inexact crime, open to extension or extrapolation. At this point in the death manuscript he added a little doubt, or critical self-reflection, into his analysis, which I appreciated, or at least noted, since there was in his thought so little evidence of it. That was one of my chief objections to his work, along with his tendency to over-reach himself and travel beyond the limits of his competence, as he imitated my thought, which was, unlike his, firmly grounded in evidence, carefully developed and worked through so that I could stand by my thought, and gather some recognition for it, unlike his thought which remained completely unrecognised and quite justifiably so. I was aware, he wrote, that I was most probably doing an injustice to medieval perception. The lack of specificity I detected in the *exempla* only looks odd from the perspective of the modern attitude, I concluded, he wrote, which reflects the assumptions of modern clinical medicine, he added. From this perspective, the perspective of modern clinical medicine, medieval *exempla* hardly talk about sickness, or not as we might understand it, since any given sickness only appears to modern perception insofar as it can be found and described in the exact tissues, or parts of the body it affects. This accounts for the near-unbridgeable gulf between the modern mind and the medieval mind. We must struggle against it, he concluded. And that was it. This was pretty much the extent of his critical self-reflection. *Whatever the difficulty*, he went on, the object of medieval attention was elsewhere. It was, I knew, he wrote, *a sickness of the soul* that the external malady was intended to signify. Medieval attention was not so much fixated on the body, the parts that suppurated, and so on, but the condition of the soul it described. If the nature of the external sickness, the secondary sickness, was outlined, this was only due to its significance as symbolic retaliation. An adulterer develops mouth cancer following the Devil's kiss in the guise of the lover. A woman is rendered incapable of giving birth because she accused the wrong man of being the father of her unborn child. A priest *has his genitalia blasted* by a thunderbolt in retribution for his fornication. A woman who takes too long to get dressed due to her vanity suffers *the devil's arse* in the mirror where her face should be, and becomes mad with it. These were some of the examples I gathered up, he wrote, alongside many others that proved my argument, and which I have now lost, but that I might with time one day retrieve, although for the present these examples must suffice to demonstrate my point, namely, he wrote, that the nature of the sickness was only specified if there was educational value in doing so, with the suffering body in question indicating an inner sickness, a soul sickness, that the body sickness was merely symbolic of. This should all be distinguished, he wrote, from Old Testament examples of divine retribution in which sickness expresses the wrath of God and has a much simpler function. I looked up again at his body. Not all of this argument was entirely that bad, I thought. After the wake I will write some of this down. I also thought that I might have read some of his writing on the island after all, when I had plenty of time to do so, although it would have been difficult to select which of the three iterations of his life's work then in my possession to begin with, for the purpose of reading, and not for comparative analysis, which required the reading of all three iterations simultaneously. But I did not know back then, as I knew now, that his writing was not all bad, although it was mostly bad and completely lacking in evidence. This hardly helped his argument. The overall lack of evidence to support his claims was actually inexcusable. With no evidence to back it up, an argument should not be made. It was of course my fault that he could marshal no evidence to support his argument, since he had been so pre-occupied by remembering it that he had no time to back-fill the references, the scholarly material to support it. But any self-respecting scholar would have gone for the evidence first, I thought. Any self-respecting scholar would reassemble the evidence before proceeding with the argument. Any self-respecting scholar would consult the evidence a second time to be absolutely sure about the argument they were remembering, to double-check each of its major points, and make adjustments where necessary in light of a fresh look at the evidence. In the medieval context, he went on, and by contrast to the function sickness has in the Old Testament, *to the medieval mind*, he added, medieval sickness no longer appears as mere evidence of the wrath of God. Sickness takes hold in order to reform the stricken body, or more precisely, the soul within the stricken body. Sickness indicates the necessity of reform and the path that reform must take. Sickness is educational, in other words. It functions as a diagnostic tool, telling the stricken and those nearby *what the learner is* from the perspective of a higher power, revealing the basic condition of the learner in a state of sickness, a condition requiring correction, where the presence of sickness indicates the basis of a course of instruction, showing what must be done, and where education must set to work. The *exempla* tradition bears this out, he wrote, as physical healing can only follow God's forgiveness, where the afflicted must follow a path to health that involves recognising the existence of a greater power, reflecting on his or her sins, feeling guilt, and resolving to change. Those featured in *exempla* as exemplary cases of transgression, cases involving sins against God, cases that were also, at the same time, examples of divine retribution, are not named, he confirmed, again without any evidence. They are nameless sufferers, he wrote, and that is important, he added, to understanding their educational function, he went on. Crucially, the nameless individuals whose stories are told are presented as near contemporaries of their audience, rather than historical figures. This contrasts with scripture, he wrote, in which those figures who appear, in scripture, and do so in their exemplary sickness, rarely remain nameless. Typically they are named, he wrote, which makes these cases less effective as stories, since the process of naming allows the listener to distance themselves from the perpetrator, given the elementary fact that they know who, precisely, it was, and can thereby supply themselves with countless reasons for why the perpetrator, the exemplary sufferer, bears no relation to themselves, and why the lesson in suffering does not translate, or extend itself to them. In medieval *exempla*, transgressors are identified by more general categories, such as social status, occupation, gender, or temperament, broad enough descriptors for the process of identification to occur, he wrote. The point, he continued, was for those in the congregation to connect with the stories as they recalled their own pain. The lesson of medieval sickness, was, ultimately, a lesson that had to be felt in pain, with every headache, in every abscess and boil. Each sufferer must make a lesson of their sickness, and wonder, in their suffering, how they might atone for bringing such violence upon themselves. As if that were not enough, he added, this economy of pain was supplemented by the possibility—itself a masterstroke of theological ambiguity—that the punishment was not actually earned, and was not retribution, and might be entirely *undeserved*, in which case it functioned more as a test of faith than as a warning or a direct prescription to behave differently. The innocent might also become stricken, and there could be a lesson in that. There is a lesson in every sickness of any kind in this educational order, he wrote. This argument is not all bad, I thought again. I might well have read it on the island. There was little else to do, after all. It was barely populated and the cottage I had been given for the purpose of retreat was barely furnished. He did not know of it, nor did I before I got there, which was crucial. He could not follow me to the cottage, as he might, given how desperate he must have been by then for contact with someone who knew him, who had known him for years, who understood the significance to him of his work and had some notion of what it included and what it hoped to achieve. He had by now rewritten his life's work three times and it would probably kill him to rewrite it a fourth, I remember thinking, although I also thought, if I remember rightly, that rewriting his life's work might be keeping him alive. Perhaps I was keeping him alive, I recall thinking, by committing him to this task, by making it impossible for him to reflect upon what his life had reduced to, because most writing, and his writing especially, serves as a distraction from how reduced the author has become, how pathetic and hopeless their life now is, which is the only explanation, really, for any sustained compulsion to authorship. Each morning on the island I woke with good intentions, deciding that today I would begin the task of comparative analysis, only the fire had long died out and would have to be rekindled first. It was too cold to read and work, my hands were stiff, I could see my breath, the cottage would have to be first warmed. This took some time as I assembled the wood, the kindling, scrunched the paper below, and stacked it ready to be lit, and then realised that I had all but run out of the middling sized pieces and would need to go to the woodshed, returning with a good haul that would then require decanting and arranging to one side of the hearth, the larger pieces above the last and largest chunks of wood from the night before that I had not quite got round to burning. With the hearth finally organised I set to work with the lighting, the blowing, the careful adding of extra kindling when needed, then the middling sized pieces, the odd curse, more blowing if necessary given my incompetence, and then finally the larger pieces until I had a good steady fire and could relax to some extent knowing that it would now not quite so easily go out on me, though fires are never entirely relaxing to be around, with their appetite for wood, and the threat that if left too long the embers will not light the next log, and will sit, smouldering, gradually cooling to ash. With my hands warmed and supple, or less stiff, if not a little dirtied, I turned to the three typed manuscripts arranged on the table by the window, which, being single glazed, was only just losing its layer of condensation which had run down too and pooled on the inner sill. Looking through the window I was able to see the track leading up to the cottage. It passed down into a hollow and then made its way up through a small, sparse arrangement of wind-swept trees, the only trees on the island, before opening out on its approach to the bit of land before the hut. There were no trees in the hollow itself, just standing water with something emerging from the swamp, but it was hardly a tree. The wood I burned was clearly imported from the mainland. It was fast-growing wood, cheap softwood with well-spaced lines grown under entirely different conditions, better than here. There was plenty of it, the woodshed was well stocked. I was the only visitor that season, apparently, so I gathered. I spent some time in the woodshed with a small axe, flinging it about, forgetting my shins, remembering my shins, feeling relief at not having cut them, making further kindling and middling sized chunks of wood and bits that flew to the side but which I didn't pick up. I hacked about in there, pointlessly at moments, and thought of him searching for the fourth iteration of his life's work, asking for me, coming to my office, arriving at my house, speaking to those who know me, bothering my daughter, worrying her needlessly, asking where I had gone, and then, finally, returning to the task of rewriting the entire thing from memory, word for word if he could, given his superstition that the placement of words was significant to the meaning of his work. All that hacking and now I had a blister. There was plenty of wood in there, more than enough. I had barely touched the extent of it. I had enough wood to sit warmed by it in the cottage for the entire day, and the day after that, or the week, returning to the woodshed to replenish supplies, day after day, reading, perhaps writing, although eating was a bit of a narrow prospect. I had not yet managed to work the stove which was not in the fireplace but sat as a separate arrangement to one side of it and away from the heat of the main fire. When I lit the thing, it smoked and sooted and finally went out. There must be an air vent, I thought, somewhere in this stove is an air vent. It must be closed, and I must open it. There is no air, it needs to open, I decided, and searched about the stove for some kind of vent but found nothing. I went away in frustration only to return moments later sure that I would find it and make the thing work. But I had no food for cooking, just bread and cheese. If I managed to light the stove it would just be another fire to look after. There was no point in lighting the stove if I could not find something to cook first. But if I don't manage to light the stove, there is no point in finding something to cook, I told myself. I ate some of the bread, and the cheese, hand wrapped in a kind of paper. The cheese was rustic-enough looking—irregular, malformed, and convincingly ugly—to be produced on the island, or so I pictured, in buckets heated over a fire, drawn out from the soup of congealed, gently heated milk, with a stick, and turned over, hand over hand, peasant hands I imagined, in a setting that was probably not as clean as one might like, drawn by the same hands that worked the udders. I had only seen sheep on the island. No cows, not yet. For the life of me I have never been able to imagine a sheep being milked. The idea of a sheep being milked has always struck me as absurd. Surely sheep cannot be milked, and yet here they are, I thought, being milked somewhere on this very island. The fire was up. It was by now essential that I had some coffee. I cannot work without coffee, I told myself, not in the morning, and although I could not figure the stove which was wood-fired and missing a vent, I could manage to heat some water directly over the fire, given the placement of a hook, a hooked chain, and a blackened kettle that even I could not fail to put into service. It was decidedly inefficient, I discovered. The whole arrangement was poor, I decided, with the hook not quite deep enough into the throat of the chimney for the kettle, when hung, to really allow the flames to lick it. Whoever placed that hook had made a mistake. I could not believe that the same person who placed the hook with a good few blows of a hammer, or perhaps just one blow, was the same person who subsequently used the hook, or if it had been the same person, surely the person who used the hook, as I used it now, always sat there lamenting the fact that they had done such a poor job, and had driven the hook, which could not be extracted, in the wrong point, lodged right into the top of the recess. The chain was also a bit short. A longer chain would have done the job better. It struck me as odd that whoever placed the first hook did not then place another, in a better spot, deeper in, just before the flue intake, learning from experience and the first attempt, which failed, where the right spot must be. And then get another chain, I thought. The hook, its position, and the failure to place another, struck me as absurd. It bothered me. And the chain, but not quite as much as the hook. I could not understand how it came to be left there, driven in like that, unless the cottage itself was absurd, was absurd in other respects, and was wrongly positioned on the island, in the worst, least productive spot, and this is why I had been led here to suffer its absurd positioning, distracted at first by the well-stocked woodshed which indicated that the cottage was valued and that the fireplace inside it made sense, which it didn't. It occurred to me that this itself was an absurd idea. We remain superstitious despite ourselves, I thought, and rocked about with that idea rattling in my head and doing nothing in particular. I sat for some time watching the kettle, looking at the spout for some evidence of steam, and then, impatiently, unhooking the kettle and removing the lid to look inside to see if any bubbles had formed at the base. It was obvious that this persistent unhooking of the kettle and removal of the lid did not help the progress of the boiling. But the waiting itself was difficult given how much I really now fancied a drink and wanted to get the water from the fire as soon as it was hot enough. By the time the coffee was brewed the condensation was gone from large parts of the window, and I sat, with the three manuscripts, looking through to the world outside, wondering about the misshapen trees, and how they managed to survive there like no other place on the island otherwise devoid of trees and tree-like plants. *The success of atonement was never guaranteed*, he wrote in the death manuscript, to *the medieval mind*, he added. I could have read those lines back on the island looking at those trees, I thought. *Taking the sacrament*, he went on, was not enough, *not in the medieval context*, he wrote. As I sat before the body, and the son, and continued to read, I thought if I might have read this on the island after all. *Pious kneeling*, or wearing a hair shirt to irritate the skin, would not guarantee God's forgiveness. Not even hair shirts augmented with twigs would work without fail, he wrote. Wear any kind of hair shirt, shove anything inside it, bleed and itch as much as you can endure, and still that will not be enough. Not even the worst hair shirts with the worst accessories worn indefinitely would do. Nothing would do. Nothing was guaranteed to secure favourable judgement, he wrote. *As the idea of Last Judgement rose to prominence* in the twelfth and thirteenth centuries, he went on, *even those who cultivated high levels of inner turmoil and contrition* could never be sure that they would be judged favourably. There was no assurance, no escape from doubt. To adapt the words of a four-teenth-century poet, he wrote, *man is born and dies in a state of infection*. The poet remained conveniently unnamed. In the medieval context it was impossible to know, he went on, if the soul will be rescued at the last moment before death, or if the soul will finally succumb to that basic infection and be eternally damned, he wrote. I wondered if his religion would now damn him too. Looking at him laid there at the wake, I wondered how he sat in relation to his religion, his second church. It was possible that he never truly believed and considered his second church to be just another establishment lie. Perhaps he only endured it because it was preferable to The Church of Christ, Scientist, which his mother had told him was a hateful religion against which the substitute church he subsequently grew up with must have seemed bland. His first church brought him up on a lie still worse than the one that would bury him, I thought. His mother deserted the first church when he was still very young but not too young for him to remember what it was like to exist within a religion, and a family setting, in which it was important to deny or at least seem to deny for the sake of appearances the reality of sickness and death. The religion she escaped to was by contrast so dry, so bland in its teachings that he hardly noticed them. That church became a kind of household furniture. It was the furniture of his upbringing. This religion was furniture by comparison with the church his mother escaped. He grew up with that religious furniture, developing, living, thinking against a backdrop he had long since stopped seeing. He was, I suspect, a Christian of that religious furni-ture only because he never made the effort to cease being one, which is how most Christians exist today, at least those of the more ordinary variety. Ordinary Christians have simply not made the effort to become something else. After The Church of Christ, Scientist, there was nothing striking about his replacement church. The church his mother fled to was uninteresting, by comparison, a creed of empty collection boxes, drab prayer books, and embroidered cushions. It was the typical church of a defeated, English Christianity, a kind of institutional Christianity that was already in the process of drying out and curling up when his family first joined and has since continued to dry up and become even more irrelevant in the decades since. Decades on, his own family had long stopped attending this church on Sundays, but would turn up for midnight mass on the eve of Christmas, suffering an obligation that would not quite die, although they told themselves and one another that they enjoyed it, staying up, sitting uncomfortably, listening to a sermon in the cold air that no longer gripped them as a church might hope to grip its congregation because the church had become mere furniture. They drew on the church out of habit. It was largely there for funeral arrangements. It offered a set of procedures and a few words. His second church was a convenient institution, providing a staged, structured plan for his death and for dealing with his body. His second church was basically a burial arrangement. Perhaps he saw no link at all between this version of Christianity which was a mere burial arrangement, and the medieval practices he spent so much time studying, or appearing to study, because he really only turned over a few commonplaces, I thought, and had nothing particularly original to offer to contemporary scholarship. Even in that form, however, the form of a few commonplaces, and hence not particularly original or surprising observations about the distinct nature of the medieval church, he failed to connect what he studied with what he was a member of, I thought. His work did not cause him to ponder the nature of the church that he still subscribed to, out of habit, and that would bury him out of habit, as if one church had not emerged from the other. Probably he would argue that the medieval church had more to say of significance regarding our present than any of the more ordinary churches now attended, since churches today are nothing but *tombs and sepulchres of God*, I thought, a little pleased with myself for recalling the quote, even if I have also now improved upon it, so I think, because a far better description of the church is that it has become a burial arrangement. Each church is at best a burial convenience, I thought, or a burial arrangement, it was hard to decide which I preferred. *Given the extent of the fall, the Fall of man*, he went on, a medieval Christian education could offer no cure.

Medieval education had definite limits and these limits were clear to all concerned. Its lessons would travel through the ears, hands, knees that received it, by way of limbs and orifices that may be used just as much by the devil. Each lesson is limited by its connection to the body, a body that is born in a state of infection. Education is tied to the body, he went on. It is limited by the fact it must perpetually address a sickness it will not solve in life. These limits were obvious to *the medieval mind*, he wrote, and in writing that, so I felt, over-reached his argument to such an extent that all he had to offer at the end of it was pure speculation. Nothing is obvious to anyone, I thought. If anything was obvious to anyone at any time nothing more would need to be said. The final examination, he wrote, *the weighing of souls*, marks the culmination and the end point of education on earth. It takes place after the body is abandoned and once it has served its function. The ultimate test of a medieval education, the decisive moment, the point at which it will be decided if education has done enough, if the body has been receptive enough to its teachings and if the individual has worked sufficiently against the state of infection, occurs once the body has finally been left behind. The final test of education happens after death, he continued, or upon death, when the dying Christian no longer has control over their vanishing faculties and becomes at best a spectator. Final judgement occurs in a realm of existence over which education has no purchase and no further influence. Medieval education breaks out in a final, concerted push for salvation as the end of education approaches, where great care must be taken, since one last error, in pride, or fear, could bring about ruin. To enter into those last moments in a state of despair, for instance, believing that the decision was already made, was just as bad as approaching death with confidence that judgement will surely be favourable. I had ceased reading, I now realised. For some sentences I had been picking words off the page and running them through my mind whilst thinking completely different thoughts. It is as if the reading bit of the brain separates from all other parts and just trundles on regardless. I find myself doing this often enough even when I am interested in what I am reading. I notice, lines, pages later, that I have not been attending to what I have been reading even though the words have been read and my eye gaze has been tracking across those words, along each line and then to the next. I realise, belatedly, that my mind has wandered, and I return, and tell myself to focus, unless what I have been reading has not struck me as worth re-reading, in which case I continue, glad of the pages I have missed, or I cease reading entirely. I had been thinking of the small misshapen trees on the island which did not yet have leaves when I saw them, and were in outline, angular, abused by wind, hardly living in fact. To the extent that they grew, they did so each year very slowly, I felt, and were probably more ancient than one might suspect. It was odd to think that these trees were likely the only ones on the island, which caused me to wonder if, in their youth, there had been others too, long since cut down. Perhaps the island was once covered in small misshapen trees, or larger trees not yet quite as misshapen as the ones I now saw, gathered for mutual protection, grown in entirely different conditions because they grew in a landscape that was shaped by trees, that existed under conditions of growth that were adjusted by those trees to the conditions that would better favour them and those they seeded and the creatures that sheltered below. Now these trees were the only ones left, I thought. They had grown in ways that were even more mutilated, with greater twists, odd angles, and aborted efforts to reach up and to the side. Each year they emerged from dormancy more hopeless, sprouting with less effort, gathering even less light. The soil was impoverished. The sap was impoverished. The shoots were already dry when they appeared each spring. There was no vigour left in these trees. As I sat at the table listening to the wood from the mainland burn, and as I looked through the windowpanes, I thought, as I recall, that I might go outside and hack away one of the limbs and burn it in the fire which by now warmed my back, or the side of it that faced the flames. The wood would smoke, I knew, being damp, and would burn reluctantly, but the fire was hot enough to consume it. One limb of that mangled growth would be gone and with it so many years of futile effort. Next in the pile on my lap was a brief survey of medieval art—representations of Last Judgement. I was able to read again, for a spell. The son had still not moved. I felt slightly refreshed as if I had slept, although I doubted it, I had no memory of nodding off. As I read, I kept the pages in the order I found them, simply out of habit, placing those I had looked at on a small table to the left, just about big enough for the pages to rest on, intended for a drink from the look of it, but now covered by the upturned, typewritten notes. He opened a new section, having moved decisively from his writing about the *exempla* tradition to the topic of Last Judgement as seen in painting and sculpture, again without sources, though I suspected that he drew in large part from one particular source, a source upon which he was not just overly reliant, but whose work he should not have turned to in the first place. I had read the work of that dubious author years ago, long before the author fell into disrepute, and still remembered enough of it to suspect that the writing of that author, now roundly dismissed by any self-respecting medievalist, lay behind much of the analysis to follow. *That author's work is dated, he did not understand the medieval mind*, as my colleagues would say. To draw on that author's work and do it so heavily was sure evidence to anyone who knew the field that the scholarship in question was poor. Authors like that are written off for a reason. Those who know what they are doing are always writing off authors and it is advisable for those who follow to write them off too. Those who know the field would not draw from that author's work, given that he *did not understand the medieval mind*. But he, of course, did draw from that questionable work and did so extensively, showing that he, too, *did not understand the medieval mind*, as my colleagues would say. Religious iconography dealing with Last Judgement, he wrote, depicts two key educational technologies, *the final examination*, and *the book of records.* This iconography represents, he went on, the passage of the soul upon death as it is materialised in medieval art. The final journey of the soul follows the end of education. The soul is separated at last from the body that can no longer be educated, because it is dead, he wrote. The reign of sickness ends at precisely the same moment since you can no longer be sick when you are dead. Education and sickness are coterminous, he went on, bounded by *the Garden of Eden* at one extremity, and *Last Judgement* at the other. Representations of Last Judgement were dominated initially, in the thirteenth century, by the idea of a divine court of justice, he wrote. There would be a set of scales, representing justice, and a throne for the judge in which Christ or God sat. In the fourteenth and fifteenth centuries another vision of Last Judgement appeared. The book or ledger replaced the set of scales. It no longer seemed that a life would be weighed up, the good deeds against the bad, since they were already recorded and accounted for. Last Judgement did not take the form of a hearing where it might be possible to plead for the soul or beg to tilt the scales. Everything is already recorded with exactitude in the book of each life, a book that is no longer a mere census like the book of lives or the book of the damned—each just a list of names— but is a book that accounts for each life individually and in close detail. This book sets down, itemises, and classifies the thoughts, words, and deeds of each individual. God is no longer modelled on the judge, or the king who rules over the court of law. God reigns over the world of men through the discipline of good bookkeeping, he wrote. This is the God of the book of records, a book of records that was, he added, a medieval form of total surveillance. I turned the page over and faced a reproduction, in black and white, of a group of skeletons clutching books. I turned over again to find a brief description, in typescript, half-way down the page. *This section is from the lower half of a fourteenth-century painting by Jacobello Alberegno. Christ sits enthroned in the top half, wearing a gilded white robe on a seat made of stone, and seems to float in mid-air. He holds a book, open to the viewer, on which is stated, HE WHOSE NAME IS WRITTEN IN THIS BOOK SHALL BE DAMNED. But the Christ figure and his book of the damned is the least interesting part*, he had written. *It is necessary to look lower down*, he added. *Lower down several souls are pictured as skeletons, each holding his own book, suffering its contents. This part*, he wrote, *is the most interesting part.* I turned the page back to face the skeletons clutching books. The skeletons on the left stand bunched together, jaws open, in a ring of fire. One points to his nose, or where his nose would have been. Those on the right wade through water towards the figure in the centre. This figure is the only skeleton without a book, standing with arms out, elbows bent, palms open, hands raised to the latitude of the clavicles. All the other skeletons gesture to, lean in, move towards, and hold their jaws open in the direction of the central figure. I turned over again. In the brief description overleaf, the one in typescript, I saw that he did not speculate on that central figure, the bookless one. He did not deal with the awkward fact that although the other skeletons held books, they all advanced towards the bookless one. The bookless one simply did not figure in his analysis even though the bookless one was right at the centre of the image that was, as he wrote, *the most interesting part.* I turned the page again and was now presented with another black and white reproduction, of an altar, with a fresco behind. I turned again to find its description. *Another similar scenario can be found on a fresco depicting Last Judgement at the Basilica of Saint Cecilia in Albi, France, painted about 150 years later, where similar booklets hang from the necks of the risen souls.* Turning back to the black and white reproduction of the fresco, I noticed that the risen souls do not even look at the book each bears about the neck, or, as it seemed to me, upon the chest. I could not actually see any evidence that they were indeed hung as described. As far as I could gather, they did not *hang from the necks of the risen souls* at all. They looked to me as though they were grafted onto the bare skin of each body, held open forever at the decisive page, each book facing outward, declaring itself to the nave of the church. The text on each book was indecipherable. Or at least on the reproduction in the death manuscript nothing could be read of each book. They seemed to have lines that imitated writing, that were an artistic representation of writing, but contained no actual words. Lower down other souls emerge from holes in the ground, naked, rising in prayer, not yet with books attached. These books presumably descend later, or appear, perhaps emerging from within the chest to become stuck there once the soul has risen. That would be even less reason, then, to read their contents, I thought. The souls rise before the books appear. Decision precedes the book, I decided. The book merely confirms the process of decision, it declares that the fact of judgement is not arbitrary, and cannot be swayed, because it is based in the infallible mandate of divine record-keeping. *This kind of book*, he wrote, or a book somewhat like it, appears again in seventeenth- and eighteenth-century baroque art, and more intimately in fifteenth-century art, as the devil holds the book at the head of the deathbed. The book is once again the symbol of irrefutable decision. It is a thing to be feared for what it must contain. Those it describes can lament the book from their deathbed and may do so without reading it, given that its contents already weigh on their conscience. The writing inside the book cannot be adjusted or edited. Each life is directly inscribed upon the page without the mediation of educated people, as readers, as writers, as interpreters. The records within each book may be intimate, but there is no relationship to be had with them, *beyond submission*, he added. Unlike the Bible and all other texts that require interpretation and must be read repeatedly by those who have been trained to read and understand them as they are to be understood, this book will not suffer disagreement or dialogue over the nature of its contents. Anticipating, indeed exceeding the high ideals of twentieth century logical positivism which would treat language as if it were a mere tool, a necessary artifice that held no interest of its own beyond its perfection as a device for communicating ideas, the medieval book of judgement has already perfected communication with the caveat that its message is only available in death and offers nothing more than decision. The medieval book of judgement contained words that were without breadth or latitude. Text and decision are identical, he wrote. The last book, the ultimate book, is not to be deciphered, it requires no mediation by the refined sensibility of the educated person. There is no room for ambiguity, no role for discrimination or taste. There is nothing to be enjoyed or relished or dwelled upon. Word is judgement, he went on. The book of judgement is to be delivered once only, he wrote. There is only one appearance of the book of judgement and that appearance is decision and does not warrant an act of reading at all, he reiterated. I had reached the bottom of the page. Medieval education obeys a trajectory unlike our own, he continued overleaf. Within each life medieval education traces its lesson as an upward curve to its final result obtained at the point of death, the absolute cut-off point for all the activity of teaching on earth. The hour of death is the last chance at redemption, the last opportunity to learn one's lesson. After death, education is no longer needed. Literacy, illiteracy, there is no distinction. There are no books in heaven or hell. After death, to be educated has no meaning, he wrote. The dream of medieval education is to know God absolutely, which only death can deliver, and once delivered, the dream is gone. This medieval educational endpoint differs markedly from that of modern education. If the hour of death is the high point in medieval education, in modernity a person's death is the point at which the activity of education has least significance. In modernity, he went on, educational effort before death makes no little or no sense. Death is preceded by a moment of final stupefaction, not redemption. Well before death, too, if death is anticipated by old age or sickness, there is a diminishing role for education, since the entire point of education in our time is tied to its ability to reproduce itself, to bring about more of the same. This is why it targets the young to the neglect of the old. *Modern education cannot see beyond its drive to self-replicate*, he emphasised. It cannot see its limits approaching given that anything outside its range of perception cannot make sense, cannot be apprehended. Anything that exceeds educational perception can only be grasped by co-option, by transforming the outside of education, a senseless realm, into the terms of educated experience. There is no outside, educated perception declares, and by that declaration speaks of its own determination not to see what it cannot understand. *Our educated perception cannot grasp the blindness it produces*, he went on. It presents itself as the condition of health, as the reason for and route to a better future, but a future that can only be imagined from within the limits of its interior. If pre-literate societies are celebrated in their healthiness, this is only because the science of educated people has valorised them. That is its profound and inexorable blindness. Educated perception, the outlook of all educated people, can only perceive what it valorises and what it co-opts by way of that co-option. This educated perception acts as its own condition of health, where to be educated is to be improved. Educated perception decides what health looks like, the health of society, of the individual, of the whole, and bestows upon itself the judgemental frame by which it judges itself. Educated perception is like a committee that decides the committee has done well. *The committee decides* that its activities have not wasted the time of its members and so it continues to do what it did before. *The committee decides* that its procedures are justifiable and important and so it does not deviate from them. *The committee decides* that it needs to reflect upon its performance this last year and judges that its performance was excellent and that it should be rewarded. The committee confirms that it is very happy with the work of its members and assigns them a bonus. At the very most, the committee does permit some doubt about its activities, about its bonuses, about its rewards, about its judgements, and about its procedures, but only on the condition that the committee or something like it continues to exist as the place where doubt is entertained and put to bed. Only the educated can know what health is, the educated decide, or declare by implication. Only the educated can perceive health, and work actively, consciously, towards it. Modern education is the condition of health and the condition of its own inspection. This is a system of value, he wrote, a mechanism so committed to its own reproduction that it cannot be seen, and will never be seen, in the extent of its self-rapture. *Our educated sensibility is sick with itself,* he declared, but understands that sickness as a sign of its health. And so it went on, his writing, the death manuscript, each statement building on the one previous but failing to meander much beyond the basic point set out many lines before. Perhaps I only read these sentences to draw attention to and confirm in my mind the inane circularity of his argument. His thought always had that tendency to turn in on itself, I remembered. Even as a child he would pose ridiculous questions that were better left ignored. As we walked to the mine, he posed ridiculous questions. As I lowered him down into the mineshaft, he went on with his ridiculous questions. As I left him there below with his ridiculous questions, they turned over on themselves and raised in pitch, but still I ignored them. Sitting here, at his wake, I remembered how in adulthood he posed questions in the very same way, with the same desperation. His thought continued like that, unproductive and anguished, unfolding and back-turning, in just the same manner as it did when I left him in the mine, as he answered his own questions, replied to his own ideas, churning them over so that they became ever more demented, the questions repeating, the ideas repeating, and the very same episodes returning, his thought turning in on itself. *Medieval education,* he continued, as I read in the death manuscript, *undoubtedly vicious in its own way,* he went on, *at least admitted its pact with sickness,* which is to say, the extent to which it was indebted to, educated out of, and in, sickness. The highest point, the apogee of medieval education, coincided with the last suffering moment of fallen Man. Medieval education ended as each life was cut to a halt. It vanished in a rising crescendo, *a last burst of commitment that coincided with the apogee of sickness. And that was it,* he wrote. There was nothing more on this page. It ended there. The idea of a rising crescendo of mental activity, *a last burst of commitment,* a final eruption of inspired thought that coincided with the moment of death, reminded me, oddly, of a superstition my maternal grandmother once had, and told me about when I was little. I recall sitting with her in her garden, listening to her talking to me about nothing much in particular until the others went out of earshot and she leant down and said, *Would you like to know something*, and I nodded back, and she said, *Well I will tell you something*, and she looked over to check if they were really gone. *I will tell you something now*, she said, *because I am also a superstitious creature*. I looked back in wonder as she said that. With the word *superstition* still on her lips she looked at me as I looked her back. *Your father's family are superstitious creatures because of their religion*, she went on, *but you can also be a superstitious creature without one*. I nodded, most probably, and said nothing, most likely stunned by the fact she had described us as *superstitious*. I kept thinking about that, the surprise of it as a term to describe us, as she continued and told me about her superstition, about an idea that she had, an idea that she could not shift, that on the point of her passing away, by which she meant the moment of her death, she would experience something uncanny, rather like a dream lasting a second, with her mind travelling further, and for one last thought-sequence, than it would ordinarily travel within the same fragment of time, filling that last second with hours of recollection and invention. She believed, so she told me, that when she died her last second would last an epoch, not in the hackneyed sense of a life flashed before me, but in the more troubling sense that thoughts not lived would occur to her, ideas she had not had would appear, and memories of events that had never taken place would present themselves, and that they would do so alongside thoughts she had lived, and ideas that she had experienced, and events she had taken part in, and people she had known. She would experience all that, all her ideas, all her inventions, in their full magnitude, and be unable to communicate them because she was about to die. This is what she told me when I was little. I looked up. The son was probably asleep, I thought. I eased the manuscript off my lap and to the floor. He did not move. I stretched one leg and then the other, my knees aching. They ache whenever I keep them set at right angles or thereabouts for any period of time. The same pain wakes me each morning from legs that have lain straight, again too long. As I wake, I wonder if I will be able to bend them. I think that each morning, even though it happens every morning, as I first experience the pain that feels as though it has locked my legs in position so they will not be bent even though I desperately need to bend them. Will I get them to bend, I wonder, and then I do. The pain builds and becomes unbearable and finally I bend my legs. They creaked, or something did, perhaps the ankle. I eased forward and gradually stood up, catching myself looking at the face of the dead father from above, then moving my gaze to his hand, and then to the floor. I made slowly for the corridor and along to the kitchen at the back of the house. The food from the wake lay there, collected in dishes. There was some coffee, cold. I boiled the kettle and watered it down, roughly a quarter hot water to three quarters cold coffee, and this made a passable drink so long as I started drinking it instantly. Drinking that and looking at the food, mounds of it, I found myself thinking again of the cottage and the trees. Some memories for no apparent reason remain sharp or feel sharp. Or strong, not sharp. It hardly matters. In any case, this was one of them, those days in the cottage, the trees in particular, and the walk at the base of the cliffs. I often think of those trees, even if all this amounts to is the memory of looking at them and the idea of going out and hacking off a piece. I did not in the end hack a limb from one of the small misshapen trees, although every morning I did consider doing so. The cottage was completely isolated. It was at the end of its track, so no onlookers if I cared about that. No reason not to hack off a limb then, although I hacked no limb that morning or any other. There was plenty of wood in the shed. Taking the track down from the cottage and into the hollow came to be a daily ritual. Sitting on the first day with the three manuscripts at the table, full of coffee and the effects of coffee, and with a small amount of bread and cheese for lunch ahead of me, I grew restless. The fire was burning well. The cottage was a mere hovel, a single room, but it was warmed, the condensation was gone, and my hands were no longer stiff. There was a good amount of day-light making its way through the window and across the small table where I sat. Under these conditions there was no decent reason not to begin the task of comparative analysis, I thought. I had a notepad, as yet untouched, and more than one pen. I picked at the various grooves, pockmarks, and scars in the wood of the table, which had suffered many different functions, I suspected, although perhaps not yet the activity of writing. As I thought about the table and its uses, I worked at the grooves with my thumbnail, easing out the softer parts of wood by tiny increments so that they fattened the region between nail and skin. This tiny amount of pressure caused me to stand up, move to the basin, and scrub out the pulp. Scrubbing below the nails has always sickened me a bit. I thought perhaps a short walk would help—it was to be a very short walk, just a bit of air and then back in again—laid a log on the fire, put on my shoes, and my coat, and made my way outside. The idea was to walk around the cottage, which I did, observing the smoke rise from the squat chimney, thinking of the warmth I had created, the light that now fell through the window. The conditions were, if not exactly ideal, at least good for the task. There was no chance of interruption, certainly not from him, and not of any other kind, or not from another person at least. These conditions would permit sustained attention and study. They were ideal conditions, in many respects. The prospect of interruption, as I have always thought, is often worse than the fact of interruption, or just as bad. When working, or attempting to work, the prospect of interruption can obliterate the ability to work so that when interruption occurs working has already stopped in any case. There was no real potential for either here, which is why the conditions were in this respect if not in others entirely perfect for the great comparative task I faced. The fire was up, the wood was assembled, the effects of coffee were running through me, and given that I was not particularly hungry, not yet, I might be able to focus sufficiently on the task that I had always put off under other circumstances, with the demands of my job and the commitments of my profession, which I could never escape, not under normal circumstances, but had entirely escaped here, having brought no other work or means of accessing it, although that was not entirely pre-meditated but was due to the haste of my departure. I had no other distractions because I left very quickly and did not take anything from my study except the three manuscripts—these were now kept in a recess behind a drawer—some pens, and a bit of paper. I had been to this island once, long ago, and was struck at the time by its inhabitants who lived a rude existence largely disconnected from the world. The island had few visitors, being small, hideous, and windswept. Arrivals were met with dull recognition or hardly that and had to struggle for the most basic amenities. Finding a place to stay and ending up in this cottage was a difficult task. As I arrived in the small port, the only port on the island, and faced their indifference, I disembarked to a social context in which my existence seemed marginalised to the point that I roamed among the inhabitants almost beyond perception. My questions and eventually my pleas were dismissed by those who passed me without faltering, as if they were barely heard. This sort of reception, which was really a kind of non-reception, would have seen most visitors return on the ferry they arrived with, that docked for two hours, unloading goods, resting against the tyres that were slung over the side of the docking area. Knowing the ways of the island from my previous visit—they suited my purposes—I persisted, eventually deciding to rest a little until the ferry left, then resuming my questions and my pleas as it became clear to the inhabitants of the port, which was barely a hamlet, that I was not returning in spite of their silence towards me, but would be here on the island for the next seven days at least, which was when the next ferry docked. Walking up and down along the jetty where the main activity of the place was now focused with the unloaded goods to be hauled away, I continued to pester them, asking for a place to stay, or for the person I should speak to about that. There was no response. As an experiment, and expecting nothing to come of it, I kicked one of the lobster cages stacked alongside into the water. Those working nearby paused for a moment and regarded me coldly before continuing their work. I left the jetty and walked up and down the only street, eventually deciding to enter the building at the end of the terrace, lit inside due to its very small windows, a building that functioned so far as I could tell as the inn. I sat and waited for those working at the jetty, the majority of the hamlet, to finish their work and filter back into the buildings that housed them, as well as to this very small inn, just a front room really, some tables, a fireplace, and a barrel on a bench at the end. The first of them arrived and, regarding me for a moment, went to the barrel, retrieved a glass from behind the bench, and poured a drink. He sat at the bench and waited. Others arrived and were each handed a glass by the landlord who emerged from the back. Later some food was brought in from the back of the house, a kind of stew, and some bread, which they picked at. I took a bowl, a piece of bread, and had some myself. There was no response. We continued to sit in that silence, which perhaps owed to my presence, until finally one said, *Take him to the cottage*. Another stood up and led me outside. As I left the inn, I was begrudgingly handed a basket containing coffee, a good-sized loaf of dark bread, and a little parcel of something else. This was the odd cheese they ate on the island, very likely produced in a room not unlike the front room I had just left. I followed the one who had been told to *Take him to the cottage* out of the village and up a rough track of lose stone and grit and eventually mud, cut at the centre or sometimes at the side by a small gully, or rivulet, it did not flow today but only gathered water from the last rain in puddles and patches. We walked for about an hour, mainly uphill, hardly inland, and did so slowly, I had luggage, I am not a fast walker in any case, never was. The track curved against the back of cliffs that rose above the hamlet. I wondered what my daughter would think if she could see me now. The track branched twice, leading once inland to the right, and once to the left in the direction of the cliffs. There was very little to observe since the island landscape was uniformly bleak, covered in tussocks of grass and rush, or what my father called swamp grass. This was until the final rise, over which the track descended into the hollow and then up to the cottage through the only group of trees, or woody vegetation, that I had seen on the island. On arrival my guide pointed to the woodshed and then opened the door to the cottage. Before I closed the door, he pointed at a tub connected to the gutter and said, *Boil it*. And that was it. Boil it, he said. And that was all he left me with. On my second circuit around the cottage on that first full day on the island, I continued to ponder the squat chimney, and the smoke, and the warmth inside to which I intended to return. I passed the window again, the one with the three manuscripts on the table below it, though I could not see them from the outside. With the intention of inspecting one of the windswept trees before returning, the closest tree, its aborted growth, to see how it twisted, failed, rotted back and set out in different directions, I abandoned the easy stroll about the cottage and followed the track as it came together, emerging from the sodden yard in which nothing grew, just a few puddles in dark mud divided between sections of better ground and surer footing. I made my way down the track, through the hollow, and over the rise, having passed the tree and forgotten to examine it. The wind was up on the other side and so I set to a bent walk down the slope to the first fork in the track and largely on impulse turned right and made for the cliff. The track turned into a gully, the wind reduced, and soon I found myself making a rapid descent through a grassy break in the precipice that became navigable by way of a blue rope, anchored by something in a tussock, probably an iron, and which I held to for security, occasionally out of necessity, working from knot to knot. For a short few moments I felt young. Then I felt old. The grass was replaced by scree from the cliff and the rope finally ended so that I made my last few strides to the base of it unaided. If only my daughter could see me now, I thought, and as I thought that I imagined her watching, and remarking, and most probably chastising me in that way she did. There was no wind here on the shore in the lee of the cliff. The tide was out. I walked to the left in the direction of the hamlet across the area between the cliff and the boulders. It was probably a good thing, I thought, that I took some air and cleared my head before embarking upon the task of comparative analysis. The fireplace did smoke a little and the air in the cottage was dank. The task I had before me was too important to begin in unfavourable conditions. It is necessary to have a clear head. The air in the cottage had actually clouded my intellect, I felt, and so I would benefit first, before working, from a good lungful of sea air. With a good lungful to think with I would return soon enough. The embers would still be hot enough to revive the fire. The cottage would again be warm, and I would begin, better disposed than before. Not many steps into my walk along the base of the cliff I came across an upturned skull. There was no jaw attached. It was the skull of a sheep. I pushed it with my toe that turned it over and saw how the front part of the skull was missing, a great hole running from the top of the head down to the nose ridge so I could look right inside the cavity where the brain and other bits must have been, which was now empty, or pretty much empty, I did not look too closely. The horns were also gone, only their roots remained at the point where they had broken off. The eye sockets were broken too due to the missing frontal region which took a section of each socket. Only the crescent of each remained. I could see down to the teeth through the hole and look at them from the perspective of their roots. Actually, there were no roots, or not as I might have imagined them. The teeth on the inside just appeared to start at their innermost part and continue outward as a uniform plane of growth. A little further on I found two vertebrae, both so well-worn and whitened that they had to be from another fallen animal washed over and turned by the sea for longer than the skull. One had wings and a ridge, at least I called them wings. The other was without wings, or what I called wings, and probably came from the neck or the lower back. The conditions at the cottage were perfect for the task ahead, I thought with my lungful of air, looking at these bones, taking another lungful, these bones which had little or no relation to the thought I was having except the relation they now had because of it. There were no books or other distractions in the cottage and I had seen none in the hamlet, at least not in the inn, with the exception of a bible, that is, and several small hardbacks on the mantlepiece which did not count. These books had either lost their spines, or their print had faded. I could not really speculate on the kind of distraction they might offer, and besides they were wedged between jars of some kind of pickle that I was loath to disturb. In the cottage there was nothing. Not even the trace of a writerly intellect. There was nothing in the soft wood that I picked at, no letters or word fragments that would distract me from the task at hand. The work of comparative analysis could only be pursued in a pure environment untouched by letters, I decided. The cottage was ideal. I had put it off for a year now, actually a year and a bit since I had been in possession of more than one manuscript. The conditions at work were not right, evidently, nor was I able to work at home where there was always something else to do. Here, on the island, I would finally interrogate his non-thought and perfect my own. As I found similar passages between the three iterations that could not have been produced, I was sure, from memory, and as I checked these against my own thought, against its structure and tone, where I would not look simply for shared arguments or points of view, but more fundamentally, for shared phraseology, sentence structure, word order, comma place-ment, and so on, what I would be looking to interrogate, in short, was the grammar of his thought which would reflect the grammar of his upbringing, the grammar of that environment and the grammar of his imprisonment in it, and would not be, so I was determined, the grammar of my own continued imprisonment, not subsequent to the analysis that I had in mind. I pocketed the vertebra with wings, dropped the other one and then continued along the coast in the direction of the hamlet which was, by my estimate, still a considerable way off. I passed several forelands without too much difficulty due to the low tide. And I made my way through the bays between them that were invariably shallow, by which I mean, each bay was not that much recessed between each foreland, sheltered no sand, and was backed by the same cliff of a hardly diminished height. I remained within the zone between cliff and boulder field where walking was easiest, with the exception of each foreland where the boulder field tended to reach the base of the cliffs, and over which I clambered, hand over foot. Eventually I rounded a more prominent headland and made down the rocks into a slightly larger, deeper bay, a bay that was more recessed than the others, placing my hand back in my pocket and turning the winged vertebra over each of my fingers. This bay had the addition of an area of rock, a platform, or floor, extending from the base of the cliff. This floor was the pavement over which the sea ran quickly at high tide, and upon which once sat the ancient cliff, now recessed, fallen, and turned to boulders. Parts of the rock floor had been eroded in turn at its weak points to form a series of pools. There was nothing much in them, just the odd stone that rounded them out each time the sea came over. The cliff behind at the centre of the bay was not sheer unlike elsewhere but had fallen away in stages with sections of earth that had slipped from the top forming mini grasslands, each existing in isolation from the next. The lowest section of cliff was stained. As I approached I saw that a small amount of water constantly fell at that point, since algae clung to the cliff reaching downward to its base. The monotony of the cliff line was broken at last, a fact that I found oddly consoling, and I paused to take it in. The fire was by now almost definitely out and the embers cooling. I would have to relight it and before that gather more kindling from the woodshed. The cottage was no longer ideal for its purpose, I felt. It was tedious, the debt I owed to that fireplace which was punishing me by my absence. Most people these days, most people I know, have a quaint idea of the delights of a fireplace, whereas every fireplace is merely a demanding, irksome arrangement, pleasurable only when there are other sources of heat to fall back on. A small movement met my eye. At the base of the algae and at the bottom of the cliff was a tiny froglet, barely having lost its tail. I could see a stump at the root of it. I had not spotted the creature at first due to the slime in which it struggled. It was clear from the effort it took that the frog would not be able to make its way back up. I looked over the top of the small section of cliff it faced, the last, lowest section down which the froglet had fallen, so I presumed, and could see a small pool before the cliff rose again, fell away, and rose again to the grassy patches higher up. In that pool at my head height there were several others of similar size, some with tail stumps, some without. They were also stranded but had a pool at least. The froglets were extremely small, they did have mouths that I could see, were largely still, and did not croak. It is a curious fact that frogs cannot jump backwards, I thought, turning the winged vertebra over in my hand. When my daughter was a little girl, she once came up to me and said, *guess what, frogs can't jump backwards*. That was her curious fact. I wrote it down. Frogs do not jump backwards, she was right, and these ones did not croak. I suspected they were still too tiny for that. Or they would only croak once I left. It hardly mattered. The only option left to them was to fall further into the bay from which there was no exit. It did occur to me that I might scoop them up, but with the froglets in my hand how far could I walk over the boulder field of each headland, I later told myself, and how far would I have to walk until there was somewhere to put them that was safe, unlike the zone in which I walked, which was saline, hostile, unwelcoming to froglets, and over which the sea would run at the next high tide and obliterate them anyway. I found myself thinking again of the fire, now diminished to ash, and continued to make my way through the bay and over the boulders at the next headland. Smaller bays followed until eventually the cliff line opened out for its last, longest section, that led towards the hamlet. I estimated that it would be another half hour before I reached the small town which was now my destination. It was in this last section of cliff that I noticed the entrances. They were square, or nearly square, and clearly artificial. It occurred to me later that these were not entrances so much as end points of tunnels that served to ventilate the network further back. The one I climbed into was much lower. I crawled past decaying props until it became dark inside. It was here that I thought about how I deliberately abandoned him, repeatedly abandoned him, down the mineshaft near where we lived, and into which we would, at other times, venture together. I crawled out backward and lowered myself down the rope to the beach noticing it was not very securely attached, but relied upon a bit of driftwood, wedged at the entrance. When I abandoned him in the mine, we were still dominated by our family religion. I did what I did against the backdrop of that religion. I coaxed him down the rope claiming to be on my way after him, to explore with him, but then hauled it up and spent the time I needed out of earshot. I had my coffee. As I left the kitchen at the back of the house, deciding not to eat any food from the wake, which lay piled up—the awful piling of food that made me sick at the sight of it—and so retreated from the kitchen, sickened by the food, and went along the corridor to the front room, I looked in and could see that the son was still asleep. I crossed the corridor and went into the study, stood at his desk, and looked to the shelf in the glass cabinet where he kept the leather volumes of his first religion, his parent's books that he found tucked away when his mother eventually died, and that he subsequently read again, he told me, and thought about at length, concluding finally, so he said, that this crackpot religion, as many had seen it, founded by the crackpot deceiver and self-deceiver, Mary Baker Eddy, was, although extreme in its teachings, not a deviant religion after all, and did not deviate from, but actually brought to expression, some of the fundamental assumptions of its age, the late nineteenth century, which are still, so he argued, related to the assumptions of our own. This religion, he told me, did not deceive us any more than the age we live in deceives us. This lying, murderous religion, as I called it, and as he repeated back to me, was no less lying or murderous than the age that pro-duced it, he said, and no less lying or murderous than the age we live in now which is related to it. There was a *Holy Bible* in that glass cabinet barely bigger than the palm, stuffed with short chunks of ribbon. It was his grandmother's bible on the father's side, as he once told me, the one who first introduced the religion to the family and

subsequently insisted on its place there. She became a regular colum-
nist in the *Christian Science Sentinel*, the weekly organ of the church,
a prominent practitioner in her local church, and a formidable force
within the family. There were three leather copies of Eddy's founding
book in the cabinet—we knew her as Mrs. Eddy when we were little—
the notorious *Science and Health with Key to the Scriptures*, all copies
again about palm-sized, his grandmother's copy, his father's copy,
and his mother's copy, so he told me. And then a whole collection of
Eddy's shorter writings, *Pulpit and Press*, *Retrospection and Introspec-
tion*, *No and Yes*, *Unity of Good*, *Christian Science versus Pantheism*, and
Poems, all written by Eddy, *Discoverer and Founder of Christian Science*
as it said on the title page of each book. There was also a *Church
Manual* first printed in 1895. Within that manual was a leaflet, larger
than the book, titled *Notes on Debate*. The first note could be read
above the edges of the book, *1. When a Member is about to speak he
shall rise and address his remarks to the Chair, and his speech shall not
exceed five minutes in duration, except with permission of the meeting*. I
drew back the glass, withdrew a book, and read a quote I knew from
Christian Science versus Pantheism. Christian Science *is* Science, *and
therefore is neither hypothetical nor dogmatical, but demonstrable, and
looms above the mists of pantheism higher than Mt. Ararat above the
deluge*. He told me on many occasions that Christian Science is a
modern religion and, as an educating force, suffers the same denial of
sickness that modern education suffers, only more acutely, more
obviously, symptomatically, and crudely. We would do well to study
Christian Science, he told me, since it reveals, despite its oddness, the
fundamental assumptions of our age. I found that all hard to bear,
given my own experience of the Church, its perversity, but he continued, The modern commitment to educational health is accompanied by a denial of sickness. Sickness can no longer perform an educational function in the positive sense by contrast to sickness in its
medieval educational context, which was relentlessly productive, he
said. As if addressing another audience behind me, he continued,
This epistemic shift is exemplified, most acutely, by the study-based
religion of Christian Science, founded in 1879 by Mary Baker Eddy. Its
presence may still be felt by many city dwellers, otherwise oblivious,
via its street-level outreach department, the Christian Science Reading

Room. We have one in the city-centre, there is one in almost every major city and town, although they are gradually, finally disappearing. Despite retaining ours, he said, it is barely visited now, I had not been there in decades, he told me, and only visited again a little while back to access back issues of the *Christian Science Sentinel* for my grandmother's articles. He told me this in his study two months ago. It seemed in rehearsal for the next annual conference, which made no sense since the conference had been cancelled. It was entirely characteristic of his thought and writing that he should still prepare for a cancelled conference, I thought. Two months ago, I sat again in the very same leather chair from which I tricked him to reveal the location of his life's work, the third iteration, concealed as it turned out under the chair itself, and gripped the arms of it, tense and frustrated that I had allowed myself to visit him and subject myself once again to the onslaught of his thought. His son had requested it, worried that his father was dangerously ill, suggesting that I might, if possible, help alleviate his mental tension, which the son identified as the reason for his father's recent decline in health, that, and his father's reluctance to eat. This was the idea, I would alleviate his tension, although I could see as I listened that his father had no intention of eating and there was nothing I could do to alleviate his mental tension with the exception of returning his manuscripts, of course, which was out of the question. Although Mrs. Eddy's book, *Science and Health*, is not scientific in any typical sense of the word, he continued, and has been viewed by many as perfectly deluded, it responds to a modernised conception of sickness, he went on. I gripped the arms of the chair, easing and releasing my grasp. Her perspective seems at first sight pre-modern in its denial of modern medicine, he said, but it has nothing to do with *the medieval mind*, he went on. You might think that Eddy's religion was a perfectly medieval religion, that it was medieval in its outlook and its hostility to modern science, he said, but Eddy's religion had absolutely nothing to do with *the medieval mind*, he repeated. Mrs. Eddy argues in a manner that is fundamentally opposed to medieval perception, he said. There is nothing medieval when it comes to Mrs. Eddy. Actually, Eddy's perspective is distinctly modern, he went on. Mrs. Eddy is a modern thinker, he said again somewhat labouring the point. For

Mrs. Eddy, modern sickness is a product of science that classifies, identifies, describes, and locates that sickness. Modern sickness for Mrs. Eddy, he said, has no existence independent of the medical gaze. Sickness, as we understand it, as she understood it, only appears to us as it does because of how, following medical science, we conceptualise and thereby perceive its presence. The leather arms buckled again under my grasp. He would have lost me by then if I had not already heard this argument before, or versions of it. He had been turning over the broader significance of Christian Science to our epoch, as he would say, for several years now, and given our shared family history he had often besieged me with his ideas concerning the Church, its teachings, and the *incredible perception despite herself*, as he put it, of its founding thinker Mrs. Eddy, and so on, etcetera. Mrs. Eddy was unbelievably perceptive, he would say. It is uncanny, he would tell me, just how perceptive Mrs. Eddy was. The incredible mental acuity of Mrs. Eddy is completely unrecognised outside the religion she founded, even though she was actually extremely perceptive and might be judged to be one of the most perceptive minds of her era. Even though everyone, anyone in their right mind, will think that Mrs. Eddy was actually insane or will think she was among the foremost deceivers and self-deceivers of the late nineteenth century, she was actually incredibly perceptive, he said. She might well be rated as one of the most extraordinary deceivers and self-deceivers of her century, of the entire century, and not only the latter part, he mused, but she must also be rated as one of the most *perceptive* deceivers and self-deceivers of that century, he continued, and that surely makes her unique. Sickness, he continued, is for Mrs. Eddy a product of the medical gaze, much indeed as Michel Foucault describes it, he told me, looking at me with that odd look he had even when we were young. He had run this argument through me before on several occasions, claiming each time, cleverly he thought, that Mrs. Eddy somehow anticipated in her century the great theoretical contribution of one of the greatest thinkers of the next century, the twentieth century, though of course Eddy was really nothing but a nineteenth century swindler, I thought, as I had always thought since I was a young man. Curiously, there is some overlap, he went on again, between Mrs. Eddy's characterization of modern medicine and that offered by the Frenchman Foucault in *The Birth of the Clinic*, which was first published, he reminded me, in 1963, almost ninety years after Mrs. Eddy's *Science and Health* published in 1875. *It might seem odd*, he conceded, to draw parallels between Mrs. Eddy, a late-nineteenth century Christian prophet, and the Frenchman Foucault, a mid-twentieth century theorist and critic of the medical gaze, he told me, but Mrs. Eddy perceived something that Foucault later theorised, he insisted, and *that* we must admit. I am sure of it, he added. I am quite sure, he said. His concession that his argument *might seem odd* was not a concession at all, I thought, but merely functioned as a rhetorical device to inflate the so-called originality and daring of his absurd claim. It pained me to listen. The leather arms of this chair will probably give way, I thought, at the seams, if this continues much longer. There is little shared ground, he went on, between Eddy and Foucault, actually it makes no sense at all to suggest that Eddy and Foucault shared anything at all. Eddy's outlook was not Foucault's outlook, and Foucault's outlook was not Eddy's, he said. When they looked at the world around them, they saw entirely different things. For Eddy, man was created in the image of God, and God is perfect, and therefore man is perfect, and so cannot be subject to illness—*it is an error of thought if you think you are ill*, he repeated. Meanwhile, for Foucault, man is an illusion or a fabrication *about to be washed away like a face drawn in sand at the edge of the sea*, as he famously wrote. And so when Foucault wrote and thought and taught, he started out from a place that was completely different from Eddy. The two of them have absolutely nothing in common and it makes no sense at all to mention them in the same breath, he said. Still, Eddy seems to already understand, he went on, and on that basis reject, the *loquacious gaze with which the doctor observes the poisonous heart of things*. This was a direct quote, from memory, of how Foucault characterised the medical gaze in *The Birth of the Clinic*. Again, I could see he thought himself very clever. Mrs. Eddy was certainly a great deceiver, he admitted, having heard me often enough make the same declaration, but she also understood the nature of medical perception in the modern age. Foucault was almost a century behind her when he wrote *The Birth of the Clinic*. She understood the medical gaze long before him. She understood it long before anyone else did, he said. The entire Church of Christ, Scientist understood the medical gaze long before the Frenchman Foucault wrote his so-called masterpiece. When Foucault wrote *The Birth of the Clinic* he merely repeated large parts of Eddy's *Science and Health with Key to the Scriptures*, or the gist of it, at least. In this respect Mrs. Eddy and The Church of Christ, Scientist, its entire congregation, anticipated the basic gist not merely of *The Birth of the Clinic*, but got, and thereby anticipated, the animating current and basic gist of French post-war theory, he added. It is a sobering thought that when Eddy wrote *Science and Health*, she already anticipated that milieu, or at least anticipated Foucault's book as an expression of that milieu. Mrs. Eddy had the medical gaze sized up long before Foucault was even born and longer still before Foucault began to think and subsequently have his so-called big idea about the medical gaze. Eddy had it all wrapped up for even longer than that, for easily a century and more before Foucault's many readers then attempted to wrap their heads around his books and wrangle over his ideas. They might have joined The Church of Christ, Scientist instead, he said. Foucault's many readers might have done themselves a favour and simply joined The Church of Christ, Scientist if they wanted to understand the medical gaze and so get the gist of Foucault's so-called big idea. The Church of Christ, Scientist may be regarded by its severest critics as a sect, as an insane cult, as a mendacious religion that kills its members by denying them access to modern medicine, but it clearly anticipated what French theory and the Frenchman Foucault would later discover and present in a more respectable garb, in a manner that intellectuals would finally accept. Mrs. Eddy defied the self-evident empiricism of modern medicine, he continued, or so I remember, and for that she is hated. But she must also be admired, he said. Even though her teachings caused so much suffering she must be admired from an intellectual standpoint. She should be admired for understanding that medical perception is not true, in any absolute sense, and offers only one way of seeing the world. She could see, he told me, how medical perception prepares the occasion of disease, and makes disease appear as it does and only as it does because of the organising principles, the conceptual frameworks, it adheres to. The sick person only appears as a sick person in the manner we now understand a sick person to be because of the medical gaze, he said. *Mrs. Eddy* refused the idea that medicine has finally cut through to the truth of things. *Mrs. Eddy* argued that medicine constructs an image of disease, he said, pointing his finger at me, and uses that image to organise empirical perception, he said, still pointing his finger, so that empirical perception feeds back into and reinforces the conceptual framework that produces it, he concluded. *Screw Eddy*, I thought, gripping the armchair, *screw Eddy and screw the Eddy influence.* Holding the chair like that I looked him back and thought how much I resented everything about my current predicament, everything he said, everything he thought, everything he represented. *Screw Eddy*, I wanted to say to him each time he said *Eddy*, or *Mrs. Eddy*. I didn't tell him that, of course. I had been invited to calm him down. I didn't tell him that because his son was so worried about his *agitated mental condition*, was worried enough to bring me here—and was in earshot—even though he knew well enough that I was busy, but still he invited me to speak to his father and take some of the heat, the inevitable build up that had occurred and must occur in a mind that races, turns over, but is never heard. This *Eddy* hypothesis had clearly been making its way backwards and forwards within his brain, never really progressing, since it was the same *Eddy* hypothesis, and the same argument in its basic characteristics that he had been repeating for some time now. His thought about *Eddy* was clearly responsible for his *agitated mental condition*, along with the fact that none would listen to his thought about *Eddy* without attempting to flee, with the exception of his son, of course, who did listen but could not appreciate his argument, having never understood why his father worked as he did or what he really worked on, something his father clearly knew because he avoided telling his one remaining son too much about his thought, just as he had avoided doing since he was a little boy, not wishing to burden the boy, his son, as he told me years ago, with the thought of an older man, he said, just as his father had not burdened him, although the reason for that, obviously enough, was that his father died young and probably had nothing much to burden him with anyway, I supposed, remembering his father as I did, his father who never struck me as particularly intelligent. Even though I was only a boy, I was never struck by his father's intelligence, it never seemed to me that his father was an intelligent man. I was probably still too young to tell but already when I looked at his father and reflected, I remember thinking, when I was about ten, or eleven, your father is not very intelligent. His father only had a year or so to live when I looked at him and thought that, and his father had no idea of course as I looked at him, and as he looked back at me, that his time was almost up. Admittedly, he said, that insight about the medical gaze, *Eddy's insight*, was concealed behind the queerness of her other teachings. She was a great deceiver, he repeated, agreeing with my own characterisation of Eddy and the religion she founded, a religion I had entirely rejected, which I decisively rejected not long after I stopped looking at his father because his father was no longer there to look at. I swiftly rejected a religion that was, he said, obviously the source of great suffering. Still, it pained me to hear him give Eddy what credit he did, particularly given what Eddy and her religion had done to his father, and countless others, who had died of neglect, as he seemed to admit, refusing themselves and one another the most basic offerings of medical science. It disgusted me, I had to admit, that he instrumentalised the suffering of his father, and then his mother, for the purposes of his argument about the nature of modern educational perception, his claim that modern education, like Christian Science, is based in the same denial, the same refusal of the presence of sickness, arguing that way, so that according to his argument, both Christian Science and modern education come from, and bear traces of, the same conceptual frame. It would be an interesting argument, perhaps, if it were not for the fact that in making it he put to work within the realm of his thought, or non-thought, the suffering of his family, where it would be better to remain quiet about that suffering, which was not simply his father's, or his mother's, but was the suffering of other relations too, as well as those known to the family who were not related, many of whom died of preventable diseases. He gathered them up, he embraced the suffering of all those he had known who died early like his father, and ruthlessly exploited them to make a point. All he did, I thought, was ruthlessly exploit the suffering of his father, his mother, his relations and their relations too, for the sake of his intellectual argument. His intellectual work, his so-called intellectual project, was not simply pitiful in its own right, but ruthlessly exploited his family history in order to give him a leg up when it came to his argument. Sickness, as Mrs. Eddy understood it, is a human construct contrary to the spiritual reality, he told me, telling me that needlessly, of course, because I already knew it. This, he said, is the basic teaching of the Church, *as you know*, where sickness is so completely divorced from the spiritual reality, indeed, that we can effectively say God had nothing to do with it, and therefore sickness does not exist. If there is sickness in the world, the Church teaches, that has nothing to do with God, and so there cannot be sickness in the world. This God, their God, our God, had absolutely nothing to do with it, and nothing to do with its nonexistence too, he said again. Consequently, sickness can no longer be taken as an expression of divine retribution. Sickness is no punishment. Sickness transmits no message. And God cannot use sickness for educational purposes. The mind, and not God, creates disease. *Disease is an image of thought externalized*, Mrs. Eddy writes. It has no reality except the reality we give it. Even preventative medicine such as the inoculation of children should be avoided, he reminded me, according to the Church, he said, since disease is the product of mental error. I knew this all well enough and from first-hand experience. Everything he said I already knew from experience because I had experienced all of it in my childhood. I knew these phrases as a child before his father died and my family left the Church. At home the life of the Christian Scientist is dominated by several stock phrases. His family used them, as did mine. *That's just error*, is one of them. I prefer not to think about the role of Christian Science in the early years of my life, and he should have found it even harder to think about, given that the church killed his father by teaching his neglect, by telling his father, effectively, as he lay ill, *that's just error*. My own father, once he finally escaped the Church, could not think about it, or chose not to, because of what it had done to those he loved. My father could not recall the Church without anger, a type of anger that was mixed with regret, if not some respect still for the extreme, unflagging commitment to the Church of his family, a confused mix which consumed him at times, or caused him to fall silent perhaps with guilt for putting me through it too, so that he did not talk about it, mostly. He told me the odd story from his own childhood, again dominated by the Church, but he did so only reluctantly and only if I probed hard enough to feel bad for bothering him. I think I never really understood the extent of deception that underpinned the Church, and how it bound its members to it, and had them make great sacrifices, given that I only experienced it as a young child, and not as a teenager, and suspect that he, too, lying dead now at the wake, across the hall in the front room, never really understood the Church either, given that he was so young when his father died, and when his mother left the Eddy sect for the English church, for the religious furniture that brought him up and would bury him tomorrow. I do recall the common phrases we used, *that's just error*, and others that functioned, so I later thought, to help assert and maintain in view the counter-intuitive teachings of the religion, such as the claim that the body and the rest of the material world is an illusion too. But really, I have no idea what it was like to live under that religion for decades, as some believers do, such as my grandmother who brought Christian Science to my own family on the paternal side, just as his grandmother brought Christian Science to his. My father fell out with the Church over a much longer period and was himself brought up in a family environment that was far more committed than the one I experienced. When he met my mother his family warned him against it, against her, against what was known euphemistically as *animal magnetism*. They told him to beware of her *animal magnetism*, or to be mindful of her *animal magnetism*, and to associate with her, if he must, without succumbing to it. The two of them were allowed to meet but only with the threat of *animal magnetism* over their heads. What happened within wedlock and between believers was surely *animal magnetism* too, I thought, although I never enquired too much about that. I really only knew what I was told. I remember my father telling me about a Christian Science lecturer from the USA and his wife (Mr. and Mrs. Mitford) who visited when my father was a boy and stayed at his mother's home. Mr. Mitford was a lecturer recognised by the Mother Church in Boston Massachusetts, my father told me, which made him a big deal, so he said. He was on a lecture tour of the UK and had been booked to speak at a venue in a nearby town, just to the north. These lectures, he told me, were supposed to be inspirational to Church members but were also made open to the public with the hope of encouraging and developing the broader membership of the movement. His mother, my grandmother, drove him and Mr. and Mrs. Mitford to the venue, a theatre in the town centre. It might have been summer, my father told me, and it may have been a Sunday, not that these details mattered particularly. The lecture lasted about an hour, he said. My father was seated with his mother clasping his hand as was usual on these occasions and also next to Mrs. Mitford. Afterwards people gathered in the foyer speaking with Mr. Mitford full of their freshly renewed faith and enthusiasm, as he put it, I recall. He said that when most of them were gone, and Mr. Mitford was still chatting to the few left behind, with my father and his mother (my grandmother) standing nearby, Mrs. Mitford went outside so he told me, to get into his mother's car which was parked across the street. There was a screech of brakes, he said, and a dull bump and perhaps a cry. They all went outside and he saw a body on the road in front of a car. It was Mrs. Mitford. Mr. Mitford, the inspirational speaker, his mother, and others, rushed out and over to her. She was conscious and moved a little, he recalled. There was a commotion around her, and my father stood some distance away. Someone spoke to the driver. I think someone spoke to the driver, he said, although he was not quite sure. Certainly, no police were called and no ambulance either. Eventually Mrs. Mitford was helped onto her feet and with support stood up. She was held, he thought, by Mr. Mitford, who was talking to her all the time and walked her to the car and lowered her into the back seat where she would sit with him, Mr. Mitford, as they were driven home. His mother drove as he sat in the front passenger seat. He told me that Mrs. Mitford had some blood on her face, her clothes were dirty, and she was obviously in some discomfort. Mr. Mitford was, he thought, praying in the back, and quoting from Mrs. Eddy's book *Science and Health*, probably phrases he was used to hearing, such as *divine love always has met and always will meet every human need*, that is to say, affirmation that we are all made in the image of God and God is perfect, and quotes from the bible like *ye shall know the truth and the truth shall make you free* etcetera. My father, who was still very young, felt a bit shaken, so he told me, and made some nervous remarks. His mother was fairly quiet. Trying to have something to say he said something about the Mitford's American accent, but the words came out as *American accident*, a terrible slip, he told me, because the accident had not occurred and they were spending the entire trip in the car denying the fact that it had occurred, or that it had precipitated any kind of injury, which it hadn't, because it couldn't, because injuries do not exist. They got back to the house and Mrs. Mitford was helped up to the first floor. She didn't say much and was obviously in pain. When in the flat he must have been kept away, so my father thought, but he did remember that they washed her face and continued to pray. She looked pale and in shock as she sat on the sofa. He went to bed. The next morning he was up later than everyone else. The Mitford's had already left, possibly by taxi. He couldn't remember whether he saw them or not. His mother must have said something along the lines that every-thing would work out, but he didn't think she said much about it because that would be considered to *make a reality of it*, a phrase we also used when I was young, although with the influence of the Church diminishing and my parents losing faith, we tended to use these phrases more when in company, if another family was visiting, for tea, perhaps, and for the sake of appearances. *Don't make a reality of it*, we would tell one another in my family, and more often in his. I recall his mother when his father was already sick telling his father, her husband, to not *make a reality of it*, words she would repeat to her son and later come to regret. *Don't make a reality of it*, they all told each other as his father fell sick. We all bore some responsibility for his sickness, or not-sickness, so I felt at the time. We had a role in his father's suffering and early death, since the Church taught, *If Jesus suffered, as the Scriptures declare, it must have been from the mentality of others; since all suffering comes from mind, not from matter, and there could be no sin or suffering in the Mind which is God.* These lines come from Eddy's, *Unity of Good*, I recall. I found those lines again in his copy of the book. The chapter is titled *Suffering from Others' Thoughts*. The implication as we all knew is that those who falter in their faith in the home of the sick must bear at least some guilt for the sickness they help produce. The boy, my father, must be kept away from Mrs. Mitford. His referral to the *American accident* was not just an unfortu-nate slip of the tongue. Her injury was in part the product of a mind that had become fixated on the incident, and so made a reality of it. *The only conscious existence in the flesh is error of some sort—sin, pain, death—a false sense of life and happiness*, Eddy writes. In the home, when facing something as banal as a cold, or as serious as cancer, the presence of bystanders is potentially dangerous. The wrong kind of sympathy can draw attention to sickness, becoming a fixation that makes a reality of it. Children must be taught not to make a reality of it. I was taught not to make a reality of it by my parents who were already losing faith yet still inflicted its perverse teachings upon their son. I recall that each time I left him in the mineshaft, hauling up the rope, I called down as he began to panic, *Don't make a reality of it. Don't make a reality of it*, I shouted at him. I looked down at him and saw the terror in his eyes as I pulled up the rope and shouted, *Don't make a reality of it*, which back then I thought very witty, but feel now, in retrospect, might have been a bit cruel. Looking back, it was cruel of me to haul up the rope and then throw down the words of our common religion, effectively declaring that his terror was a false terror, that he was suffering from a belief in that terror, and that was why he was terrified and should not be terrified because he would not experience terror, the pain of it, if he could only not *make a reality of it* and be contented down there in the light of his religion. But what I did to him, there, I think, can be understood, even if it cannot be excused. What I did was understandable in the circumstances. It was my parent's loss of faith which I hurled down at him and to the dark tunnels and chambers beyond. It was because of my own parent's loss of faith that I shouted to him, stuck down there and clearly terrified, to *not make a reality of it.* As I told him that, I had good reason to do so. I was just working things through in my mind. I was distressed by the religion just as much as he was, if not more so, a religion that had us live at such personal cost even if it was also a distinctly loving religion, there was a strong element of love in that religion, a warmth that held the Church community together. We were not allowed to suffer, and so I had to see him suffer. We could not experience pain without believing it was error, and so I had to see what pain looked like without that belief. As he looked up at me, his pain looked too, he was sick with his fear which was his pain, and I could see the presence of sickness, the suffering of his eyes. This religion taught us that I should not see what I saw. It taught death is illusion, the body does not exist, and sickness cannot afflict us. Even the most basic medicines endanger health by fixating the mind on the unreality of pain, it taught. Taking aspirin is error. My parents and his, and the other families we knew, did give themselves some leeway in severe cases of ill-health, as I remember, because we had a phrase for it, *You've got to take the human footsteps*, we said. It's not like we're Jehovah's Witnesses, we would say. We're not Jehovah's Witnesses, is how we would introduce ourselves outside our religion. The teachings are strict, but we aren't Jehovah's Witnesses. Ours is a distinctive religion and what others might perceive as an outsider religion, but we were hardly Jehovah's Witnesses, is how we felt. Ideally only bandaging and so-called *making comfortable* was permitted, but we were not dogmatists and would say to one another, *You've got to take the human footsteps* when we resorted to any kind of medicine, guiltily, of course, because medical care is to be considered dangerous as Mrs. Eddy taught us, since *faith in rules of health or in drugs begets and fosters disease by attracting the mind to the subject of sickness*. Some of us did seek medical attention when more severely ill. But a trip to hospital was always delayed as we prayed against our false belief in the sickness that afflicted us. *It's just error*, we would tell one another and ourselves. But eventually many did finally relent and find themselves a doctor, where it was the delay itself, rather than complete, radical abstinence, that would eventually kill those who subsequently died of their belief in a growth, or their belief in a pain in the chest, or their belief in the taste of blood in the mouth, and so on. It was the delay that killed the people I knew and the people I heard about, so I remember, those who turned away from their sickness and continued to do so until it was too late. They eventually relented and sought medical care when there was nothing that could be done any more to save them. And when those doctors they finally met witnessed the effects of their denial, those very doctors acted the role of their importance, subjecting Church patients who were too ill to the knife when it was kindest to let them alone and to their religion. *As you know*, he said, the sick must turn away from sickness rather than to it for their instruction since *to admit that you are sick renders your case less curable*. He quoted those words to me as I sat there suffering his analysis, sitting there only because his son had demanded I come to calm his father down, sitting before him, suffering his thought, suffering his *agitated mental condition*, as his son called it, as he told me, as the man told me, *This would seem* to overturn or perhaps sublimate centuries of educational effort, both Christian and pagan, that has based itself within an explicit discourse of sickness. Mrs. Eddy appears here, he said, in this teaching, to revolutionise educational perception, he told me. Or, more exactly, he said, correcting himself, Mrs. Eddy appears here to reflect a revolution in educational perception. She was perceptive enough to reflect that revolution in the religion she founded, he clarified. Mrs. Eddy was a perfect expression of her century, he said. Eddy was a nineteenth century phenomenon. She reflected in her thought the thought of her era. Eddy was not the survival of belief, or superstition. What Mrs. Eddy taught us, she taught from the perspective of the nineteenth century, from the entirely modern perspective of that century, he said. These Eddy teachings must be contrasted absolutely from those that preceded them, since Eddy entirely reversed the order of things, he went on, or at least reflected a complete reversal taking place about her. Consider the second century physician Galen, for instance, he said. Galen was an ancient thinker and reflected a resolutely ancient way of seeing. Galen argued that admitting one's sickness was a necessary precursor to becoming educated. According to Galen, conceding sickness, admitting how sick one was in both soul and body, was the point at which the person to be educated recognised that they were in need of instruction, that they were *sick enough for it*. A century earlier, he continued, the Stoic, Musonius Rufus, taught pretty much the same thing when he said, *The school of a philosopher is a hospital. When you leave, you should have suffered, not enjoyed yourself.* Just imagine if schools demanded this today, he said, and asked each pupil as they exited, *You have suffered, yes, but how badly did you suffer, how would you quantify the suffering you felt, which words would best describe that suffering, because you should suffer each day, it is good to suffer, you must learn to suffer and suffer well.* That's effectively what old Musonius taught, isn't it, he said. Because that, surely, is what he meant, he told me, looking at me for some kind of response. At least when you went to hospital, he said, you suffered, he told me, and you did so as a profoundly sick man, he added, that is to say you suffered acutely. But when you went to hospital you did not treat it as a school, he went on. You only knew how to suffer in medical terms, as I recall, he said.

I did not respond to this, to his biographical opportunism. I knew the Stoic line of course, it is recorded by the philosopher's student, Epictetus, and this gives it a special twist, as I have often thought. It gave the line a special twist to say that, *when you leave*, as his student wrote, *you should have suffered, not enjoyed yourself.* I have often thought about that line, and here he was now quoting it back to me. The most famous example, he went on, perhaps thinking I was impressed by his intellectual reach, the one that sets the trend, is that of Socrates whom Plato likens to a midwife. Socrates, it seems, must ease the philosopher-student through the pains of philosophical labour. There is no education without a good measure of sickness, he concluded, a lesson medieval education takes and runs with. As I listened to this, I did not mention the fact he'd just likened the pains of childbirth, employed here as a metaphor for intellectual production, to sickness. This was a good example of the carelessness of his thought, I felt. It was just like him to conflate childbirth with sickness. This age-old position on sickness, he went on, as I gripped the armchair, on the necessity of attending to it, and on the importance of pain in the processes of learning and self-formation, was prominent within pagan philosophy, just as it was the founding move of Christian asceticism and medieval Christian education after that, he added. Our modern departure from this explicitly recognised role of educational suffering is, he said, as radical as it is unacknowledged. For Eddy, who presents this departure in its loudest, most obviously disavowed form, the sick must heal themselves by ignoring rather than engaging with their ill health. This is why Eddy is resolutely modern, he said. Pain is just another illusion. Pain must be denied. Pain does not exist as something to be remedied and pain does not teach anything worth learning as Eddy taught us. If you can *mentally unsee the disease, then you will not feel it, and it is destroyed*, she wrote. Against the common phrase, listen to your body, Christian Science teaches its followers to *silence the body*, he said. I faltered in my recollections and listened across the hall. In this room it was hard not to recollect what he told me when I visited. I was reminded of it as a consequence of retreating to this room. Because I no longer sat with his body, I was brought to recollect what he said to me here in his study. Finding myself in his study, I saw myself recalling what he told

me, the words he used, the phrases he chose, as I sat, back then, gripping the arms of the chair, wishing that the son had not bothered me
about his *agitated mental condition*. My memories of sitting there
returned to me now, and I abused myself with them. This is remarkably common, the return of memories to the mind as agents of
self-inflicted psychological abuse. It happens all the time. As I sat,
knowing there was nothing that I could do to relieve his *agitated
mental condition* with the exception of the one thing I could do but
chose not to, he went on and on as his son listened from the hall,
hoping that I might do something about his father's condition and so
allow his father the space to eat and to drink. This particular Eddy
teaching about the need to *silence the body* may sound recognisably
Platonic, I remember his father saying, or something along those
lines, and thus what I am claiming here might at first sight appear
continuous with pre-modern education in that Eddy too, like Plato,
rejects the body, or dismisses it as the source of error and distraction.
And yet, he continued, Platonic philosophy sought also to train the
body. Early Christian ascetics would also listen to the body and submit
it to discipline and instruction in order to overcome its distractions,
clearly differing in their teaching and practice from the flat denial of
the body and its problems by Eddy's Christian Science. For early
Christians, he said, paraphrasing something I had once written, so I
thought, the body was a training ground for the soul. Early Christian
ascetic practices such as fasting were intended to reconstitute the self
so that body and soul would no longer be enslaved to the appetites.
Even illness was considered profitable by these Christian opportun-
ists. *You must consider your illness a pedagogue*, Clement of Alexandria
said, *which leads you to what is profitable to you—that is, teaches you to
despise the body and corporeal things*, because the body *is the source of
worries, and is perishable. This life down below—as Plato says—is a
training for death. If you philosophize in this way, you will teach many
people to philosophize in their suffering.* The body might have been
loathsome from this perspective, from Clement's perspective, I
remember him telling me, but it was the best educational tool one
had, he emphasised, looking at me, knowingly, I thought. I wondered,
as he quoted these lines, where I had written them. Surely these lines
were largely my own, and if some of it was not, since the quotations

themselves were not mine, their selection nonetheless was my doing, so I felt. Clement's lines had been widely available for centuries, but *he* had still taken them from me, and not from Clement. He had taken these lines from my own writing, I was sure of that, and so it was entirely justified that I felt possessive over them. I was sure that I had written these lines down some time ago and published them before he adopted them. I had taken them from another source long before he took them from me, which made them effectively my lines, or at least mine before they were his. Certainly, the quote was one I was familiar with, and had pondered independently without the flavour of his thought influencing my own. I began to suspect as I sat there in the leather armchair that he paraphrased my writing more often than I realised. I have written so much, over so many years, I forget even the titles of the works I have written let alone their contents. It was possible that he quoted my words back to me and that I, given my distaste for his thought or non-thought, failed to identify them as my own. It was curious to think that by paraphrasing my work in a context I could not recognise he had managed to alienate me from ideas that were legitimately my own and that I had once felt, and worse than that, once *believed*, yet could no longer identify in the context of his presence and his co-option. Words from his mouth sounded so different than words from mine. The focus of Eddy's Christian Science is all on the mind, I remember him saying, although I have started to wonder just what exactly I am recollecting. As taught by Mrs. Eddy *whose only work*, she declared, *is the work of love in the helping of mankind to help themselves*, the Christian Scientist must be mind-positive, he told me, looking for some kind of reaction. I did not react but just sat there grasping the arms of the chair. Mrs. Eddy, he said, was *the pioneer of the mind cure*, she was *the pioneer of the mind cure*, he repeated, since I had not even raised an eyebrow, she pioneered the attitude that denies that failure is inevitable, he said, which refuses to dwell upon pain or negativity and insists that all shortcomings can be overcome by submitting to the logic of improvement, and the spirit of hope, he added, looking at me again for some kind of reaction. By contrast, medicine, for Eddy, is entirely negative. Medicine sees sickness as the inevitable state of humankind. Medicine is abhorrent from Mrs. Eddy's perspective, he said. It is profoundly negative. Medicine is

driven by negativity. It is a negative force, he went on. Medicine finds
new grades of sickness everywhere, it discovers entirely new categories of sickness all the time, new pathogens, and viruses, and so on, as
well as fresh diagnoses for the mind, so many more each decade, mul-
tiplying the categories through which we can be viewed as sick and
see ourselves as sick and ailing creatures. It looks everywhere for
signs of sickness and then finds them everywhere, he went on, ven-
triloquising the Church teachings he no longer believed. Medicine
declares that its best hope actually lies with finding sickness in apparently healthy people, so that each sickness can be treated in advance.
Medicine, he went on, is persistently, pathologically negative,
whereas Mrs. Eddy, he continued, has to be seen as the first positive
psychologist, of sorts, where all positive psychologists, he told me,
are only ever pseudo-psychologists, and have nothing much to do
with mainstream medical science. She was before her time in many
respects, placing the mind cure at the core of her religion, he said. I
think I looked unimpressed rather than simply blank and perhaps this
is when I finally relented from sitting in the leather chair, and stood
up, wondering just how much of this I had to endure for the sake of
his son, who feared for his father in his state of agitation, in his *agitated mental condition* which hardly struck me as more acute than
normal, although given his overall state of malnourishment, the hol-
lowness of his cheeks that puffed out every so often as he spoke, and
his eyes, which seemed recessed, if only slightly, and perhaps it was
only the lighting in his study that recessed his eyes, he did appear
worse as he shook with the words he spoke. I went to the window and
stared outside. Suspecting that all this stuff about Eddy as a pioneer,
somehow, of positive psychology, had not impressed me in the
slightest, he switched to his next grand hypothesis. Mrs. Eddy, he
said, also bears important traits of the modern progressive educator,
a claim of his that was by no means intended to flatter Eddy, since he
held the educator in contempt just as he held, or appeared to hold,
Mrs. Eddy in contempt. He held Eddy in contempt insofar as Eddy was
symptomatic of educated modernity. According to this logic, to the
extent that Eddy was an expression of modern thinking, of the modern
educated outlook which he despised, Eddy should be despised. When
Eddy anticipated positive psychology—the substitute-religion of

modern secular living—this observation was a strike against Eddy just as it was a strike against positive psychology. And when Eddy came to resemble the progressive educator, the implication, clearly enough, was that Eddy was as bad as the progressive educator and the progressive educator was as bad as Eddy. This is how his argument progressed, linking one to the other, and denouncing each by association. The wonderful thing about Eddy, the great gift of Eddy's example, for him, is that Eddy symptomized everything more obviously, more grotesquely, so that associating anything with Eddy was an easy way of denouncing it. This is what he found so delicious about Eddy, and that is why he enjoyed thinking so much about Eddy, I thought. He took so much pleasure in denouncing everything by its Eddy association that he almost appeared to side with Eddy for presenting him with such a delicious opportunity to denounce others. His love of Eddy, so I thought, was a consequence of how he used Eddy as his destroyer, a weapon hateful in itself but wonderful for the destruction it might cause. Even though I stood at the window now, and could not look more disinterested, he persisted with his argument. Practitioners figure prominently in Christian Science, he went on, but its founding text is considered to have healing properties of its own. All of which I knew. He was not addressing me at all, but continued to rehearse his argument for another audience. Eddy's book, *Science and Health*, can heal without mediation, he said. Its achievements are testified at length in the final chapter, the *Fruitage*, that was appended to later editions. I was familiar with this last chapter too, of course. It is a huge appendage running to more than a hundred pages, as I remembered rightly, made up of an edited selection of letters originally sent to *The Christian Science Journal* and *Christian Science Sentinel*, which between them continue to publish testimonies written to much the same formula, so that there are now thousands of so-called miracles recorded and set down as if they offered irrefutable evidence of the healing powers of the religion, or sect, and the obsolescence of medical science. Vast numbers of ailing souls have been cured, this great appendage declares, and they have been cured through the perusal or study of the book in which the *Fruitage* appears. I walked out to the hall and looked into the front room. The son was still asleep. Although I did not want him to wake and find me gone, I could not persuade myself, quite yet, to return to my seat by his father's body. This would involve picking up his manuscript, left on the seat, and would entail looking at it for the sake of the son, or simply to avoid looking at his father. I returned to the kitchen, heated another coffee, one-part boiled water to three-parts cold coffee, a passable drink if drunk almost instantly, and sat in the study, not on the leather armchair since I would surely fall asleep, but on the edge of his desk where I would not, and to pass the time took one of the small editions of *Science and Health* from the shelf to peruse the final appended chapter, the so-called *Fruitage.* Cured ailments, as I read, include cataracts, astigmatism, the need to wear glasses whilst reading *Science and Health*—eye problems are among the most frequently mentioned complaint, I noticed—smoking, *a smoker's heart*, drinking, a bad back, spinal disease, a liver complaint, a cold, bilious attacks, laryngitis, eczema, bunions, diseases that would cause a physician to remark openly *What keeps her alive?*, the need of a Mother, recourse to opiates, egotism, selfishness, hereditary deafness, *catarrh of the head*, *catarrh of the stomach*, chronic catarrh, catarrh and sore throat, *constipation in its worst form*, acute bowel trouble, obstinate stomach trouble, *a morbid fear of food*—healed by a quote from *Science and Health* which declares *neither food nor the stomach, without the consent of mortal mind, can make one suffer*—kidney trouble, bladder trouble, hernia, scrofula, peritonitis, asthma, tuberculosis, being looked upon sadly for being an atheist, having once been *an outspoken infidel*, fatigue, nervous headache, too many liver spots, insanity, *darkness and gloom*, the desire to commit suicide, insomnia, profanity, such thoughts as malice, revenge, etcetera, other facial blemishes, depraved appetites, *all that flesh is heir to, a loss in flesh of sixty pounds*, ruined teeth, a broken jaw, rheumatism, bronchitis, croup, measles, whooping-cough, tonsillitis, fever in children, other problems childhood presents—*I have five small children, and Christian Science is invaluable to me in controlling them*, indeed, *they often help themselves and each other to destroy their little hurts and fears*—crooked limbs, *lungs like wet paper*, consumption, cancer, time spent in hospital, corns, the idea of being operated on a second time, a life that *was one ceaseless torture*, a multitude of ailments, neuralgia, heart disease, disagreement between doctors, a dislocated shoulder, a sprained ankle, falling out of love with one's sinful husband—*Go home and see only God's perfect man, you don't need to love a sinful mortal such as you have been looking upon*—failure to understand the Bible, not realising there is but one Mind, the inability to *prove all things*, dropsy, yellow fever, headaches, *headaches caused from female trouble*, pains of childbirth, *darkened consciousness*, and finally, being *a follower of Voltaire*. All this appears in the *Fruitage*. I have not made it up. It is an extraordinary appendage to Eddy's *Science and Health* as I have often thought. As a young child, though I did not have the words, I was struck by how strange it was that such a vast array of ailments ranging from terminal illnesses to slight irritations are presented on the same narrative plane. Of course, from the perspective of Christian Science, all afflictions listed in its copious testimonials are alike in their non-existence, a scratch is equivalent to a heart attack, a bump is the same as a severed finger. All testimonials attest to the power of the book. *The Spirit of truth which inspired this book was my physician*, one reports. As the *Fruitage* demonstrates, the lessons of Christian Science can be taken up through individual study, by time spent alone with *Science and Health*. As a study environment, so I remember, he said, weekly church services supported self-directed learning by setting some of its expectations. On Sunday the service was led by designated Readers, not priests who would have privileged access to truth, he said, just Readers. On Wednesday evenings, volunteered testimonials from the week just gone reasserted the *Fruitage* of Christian Science and the benefits of staying with, and repeatedly reading, *Science and Health*, the ultimate *textbook ... the voice of Truth to this age*, as Eddy writes. I knew all that. I understood the context of the religion only too well, but he took it much further, seeking, as he did so, to explain how Christian Science symptomizes certain presuppositions of our age. In its conception of study, he said, Christian Science works towards and upholds a version of the post-Enlightenment educational ideal, which is the ideal of the independent, self-directed, self-realising learner who works under the guidance of similarly inclined teachers, that is to say, teachers who are also independent, self-directed, and self-realising, and exemplify those traits for the benefit of their students. These teachers are guided by the idea, he said, quoting Eddy, that *every man will be his own physician, and Truth will be the universal panacea.* Christian Science education, like its post-Enlightenment analogue, sets out a stall on which, as Eddy writes, *its pharmacy is moral, and its medicine is intellectual and spiritual.* I stood at the window, my back to him, wondering how much longer I would suffer his analysis before turning to tell him abruptly, *I am leaving,* since there was no gentle exit from his thought and the onslaught of his so-called analysis. I remained silent and so he went on, Modern education, in its liberal and progressive forms, modern teachers who consider themselves liberals, or progressives, or those who have no name for themselves but are clearly unflinching humanists, preach tolerance for other creeds and points of view, *as does Christian Science,* he said, and I could hear his cheeks billow with it. Mrs. Eddy argues the point a little bluntly, admittedly, he said. Eddy writes that others should be left to make their own mistakes, because these mistakes will eventually *open their blind eyes.* Hardly an example of liberal tolerance, I thought, that line of Eddy's to *open their blind eyes.* Precisely an example of liberal tolerance, I suspect he felt. But he went on, claiming that Eddy also sides against indoctrination, which is, after all, the flogging horse of liberal educational thought. How can we teach others, he said, and tell them what they need to know but not indoctrinate them in doing so, it asks itself endlessly, in a line of argument that has always bored me too, a problem that so-called liberal educators present themselves with, and appear to seriously consider, asking themselves how exactly the educator will solve this thorny, impossible problem of teaching others out of their ignorance whilst not indoctrinating them in the process. Mrs. Eddy, he argued, sides against indoctrination because she addresses her teaching to willing students only. On no other basis, Eddy writes, will the teacher *unfold the latent energies and capacities for good in your pupil.* Didactic and overbearing teaching is rejected, *The sick are not healed merely by declaring there is no sickness, but by knowing that there is none,* she writes, and so Mrs. Eddy is aligned once more with the progressive pedagogue, he said, to my back. For Eddy, didactic teaching is the antithesis of good practice. All good progressives, the most sanctimonious of all educators, he said, argue against didactic teaching, and say, *that* is mere transmission from teacher to student, and *that* doesn't work anyway, and *that* destroys the spirit of teaching, and so on. There is little to distinguish Eddy here from the broad current of progressive educational thought, he repeated, since *the sick are not healed merely by declaring there is no sickness, but by knowing that there is none*, to quote Eddy. You cannot be told what you must know, progressives argue, you must discover for yourself what you need to know, what the educator feels you will benefit from knowing. Isn't this precisely what Christian Science teaches, he went on as I stood at the window. Eddy also goes on about *man's individual right of self-government*, the basic principle of liberal thought, after all, he said, where it is only justifiable to infringe on the freedom of others, on their right to self-government, if it is to their benefit. When Eddy goes on about *man's individual right of self-government*, she supports one of the cornerstones of liberal thought, he said, and reveals that this *right of self-government* has always been a pseudo-right, a right to self-government that can only appear and be taken up within definite parameters. Teachers abuse their pupils because of that *individual right to self-government*, he said. They say that what they do is to their benefit, to the benefit of their pupils, and as they do so they abuse them. They say that just as they abuse them to justify all the abuse they enact. Mrs. Eddy writes how the Christian Science teacher has *no moral right to attempt to influence the thoughts of others, except it be to benefit them*. Here too we find a basic element of post-Enlightenment education, he said, now formulated as its exemplary paradox, where educational thought can only justify its interventions, its intrusions, on the basis of that assumption, where educators must believe that what they do is somehow, fundamentally beneficial. Kind-hearted educators basically imprison children, they keep them in holding pens called schools, and only live with what they do because they think it is to their benefit. Liberal and progressive education, he went on, has to assume that it is fundamentally beneficial, that its motives are basically good, in order to exist within the institutional machinery of modern education which is nothing short of a means to imprisonment. As he said all this, he did nuance his analysis, I thought, and perhaps this is why I still remained there, and did not say, quite yet, *I am leaving*, arguing as he did that none of this should be taken to imply that Eddy's Christian Science teaching and modern secular education are alike in all respects. Mrs. Eddy, he said, would find many features of modern secular education problematic. She might argue, for instance, that today's education produces too much *mad ambition*, as she called it, or that today's education is based on the obliteration of a spiritual realm where teaching, as she conceives of it, would meaningfully take hold. But here she would agree with most educational critics who claim that the problem with education, today, is that it has been instrumentalised to such an extent that the educational *good* is squeezed out of existence. Christian Science and modern education still occupy a similar space, he repeated, converging in their attitude to and denial of sickness, a denial that is connected to an idealization of the Mind and its capacity to generate the condition of health. What else, indeed, underpins the sentiment of educated people, he asked, but the conviction that *if only more were like them*, things would be better. This, surely, he said, represents an idealization of Mind on a par with the mendacity, as you might call it, of Mary Baker Eddy and the Mother Church. Both Eddy and the educated person believe that the Mind is the means to redemption. But nobody will see this as I see it, he said. *The unflinching commitment to education of educated people has to be one of the most lamentably unquestioned presuppositions of our age*, he declared. I returned to the son and his father, forgetting, I think, to put the leather-bound volumes back in the glass cabinet. I did eventually say, *I am leaving*. My departure was necessarily abrupt. I cannot say how he looked because I did not look over as I left the study and met his son in the front room where he had been waiting. I told his son that he need not worry. Your father is on top form, I said, without a hint of irony, and impressed myself with the show I put on in front of his son for the son's benefit. It was strange to think as I sat back down in the chair, facing the father and the son, that not two months later I was here again in the front room putting on a show for the sake of the son. There was nothing that could have been done for the frogs, I thought, sitting back down in the front room where the son was fortunately still asleep, his head bent forward, observing nothing. I had nothing with me that I might put them in and there is only so far that I could walk with my hands cupped, frogs inside, before they fell or jumped out. It was a kindness to leave them where they were, I decided, to face a single trauma, the rising tide, and not two or more traumatic experiences, beginning with me attempting to save them, stressing them as I walked, and eventually dropping them, or them hopping out. I should not feel bad about the frogs, I thought. It was a good thing leaving them there, that first day at the cottage. There is no sense feeling bad about them, or even remembering them. It was ridiculous, me sparing a single thought for the frogs. They were only worth remembering as a distraction, since I was now, as before, facing the side of his head, staring into his ear, wishing I had not been so weak, so susceptible to conscience, to have offered to sit with the son until morning. I thought now as I thought then that I might well have lifted the fallen froglet and placed it in the pool with its companions further up the cliff. But extracting it from the algae might have been difficult, it was entangled, and they were all destined to fall, I sup-posed, at some point, and there was no point in making this one fall twice. The son stirred a bit. After the mineshaft in the cliff, I walked more definitely along the shore, turning the winged vertebra over in my pocket, tired of the terrain for some time by then, turning the vertebra over, wearied of how small rocks and shingle yield with each step defeating each stride. Sand is the same, pleasurable for the first few steps but soon tiresome and eventually completely irksome. The hamlet approached, it gained slowly due to the terrain, until, with my calves done in, my feet too, I walked into town along its only street and faced as before the same indifference and near complete disre-gard of my presence as if I hardly existed, at least not to them. I first visited this island years ago, having read the report of a colleague of mine who conducted fieldwork there, studying the population, about which she drew no firm conclusions, but she did describe the same feeling I now experienced on entering the town. Having read many other reports of other field settings that my colleague had written, I was struck by the fact that on this occasion there was no explanation, no theorisation, just description, as if the abjection my colleague was met with could not be deciphered by the words that her academic dis-cipline made available to her. I went on that first visit out of curiosity, faced a similar level of disregard, and left on the same ferry I arrived with. My second visit was not a function of my curiosity, but the opposite. I chose the island because it would not yield to my curiosity, as it did not yield to the ethnographer's curiosity, an expert who could make no sense of what she saw and experienced, in particular their attitude to the arrival of a stranger, such as the ethnographer, or such as myself. The ethnographer justified her decision, so I recall, to only describe and not seek to explain or theorise what she saw, by writing, *When a social reality, an organising totality, remains beyond explanation as this community surely did, as do many other communities, I suspect, the only task remaining is to describe what is perceived, to diligently, patiently describe the full absurdity of what has been witnessed, rendering it so ruthlessly, so exactingly in print, any reader cannot fail to also feel a disturbance of the apparatus of sense-making.* For my part, I had barely any interest in the island on my second visit and wished only to navigate it in the most basic way. I was determined that the island would not disturb the activity of my own particular sense-making and my hard-won intellectual independence. I also happened to doubt the ethnographer's art, I have to add, but that is a separate matter. The conditions were, I felt, perfect for the kind of work I had in mind, for which I would still prefer to have the benefits of civilization, food, shelter, and so on, but wished to spend some time without any kind of interruption, or even if I did not entirely manage to avoid interruption, without any kind of regard for what I was doing. I knew that on this island I could study and work without needing to think about what others were thinking or working on, or what they were thinking about what I was working on, since those who lived on this island seemed unable to devote more than the absolute minimum attention to my presence. Given the high concentration my work would require, it was essential that I could pursue that work without interruption or fear of interruption which can amount to the same thing as I have always thought. Nonetheless, being on the island had started to irk me, so that if the ferry had been in port, I might well have boarded, even without the three manuscripts or my belongings. I have no love of ferries, or aircraft. Trains less so. Each is effectively a prison where the passenger gives up their liberty on boarding and only receives it back once they are allowed to disembark. This imprisonment becomes obvious to the passenger if there is some kind of delay, even just minutes before the gangway engages and the gate opens, whereafter those on board feel trapped, if only for a moment, and which they soon forget, of course, or nobody would embark as often as they do on ships, and planes. Cruise ships are effectively great prison complexes disguised as pleasure boats, so that those on board do not realise how much they have paid to give up their liberty, and how acute their confinement has become. I always board reluctantly and face my inevitable imprisonment considering my confinement a necessity I must put up with in order to travel from one place to the next. I am entering this sea prison or this sky prison willingly, I think, because it is necessary to submit myself to imprisonment if I want to get to where I wish to be. The island was its own prison, of course, for the seven-day period between one ferry departing and the next arriving. And it worked. I did not worry that he might turn up as he bothered me at my office and in my home. The islanders left me alone. His manuscripts were now laid out, all three of them, and ready for inspection. The walk from the cottage had been much longer than planned—just a short stroll, twice, or a maximum three times round the cottage before I returned. I would have put another log on the fire and so benefit from my efforts that morning to light the thing, and bring it up to a decent temperature, and then mess about with the kettle, and the chain, which was too short and hung from a hook that made no sense. But I walked to the shore instead and now it was too late. The fire was certainly gone, the ash pile too cool to revive, so that I would have to start it again. The walk back to the cottage was a long one, even the quicker route which was the land route and the only option really given how much I hated the thought of returning to the shingle, the sand, the boulders, going along the shore from one bay to the next, and so I would definitely travel up the track above the cliff and make my way along it as I had done on the first day, as I followed the islander who took me as commanded but did nothing else, did not even look at me, although he did say, *Boil it*, when we arrived, which was helpful. It would not be hard to follow that track. There were only two forks, the first leading inland and the second to the cliff that I had taken that morning. But if I left the hamlet now, I would not be back before mid-afternoon, I suspected, and so would arrive with not that many hours of light left given the time of year. By then the conditions would be too poor to study and begin the task of comparative analysis. There were some candles in the hut, but it is not possible to read by candlelight, only quaint. Nobody reads by candlelight,

I thought, they just pretend to and look at themselves and think how quaint they are in doing so. It would be another day before I returned to the manuscripts, a long night breathing vapour in the bed, just a cot at one corner of the room, a room that was the extent of the hovel, the fire cooling if I did light it again, and my toes finally feeling the cold as the temperature dropped. Then my hands. And neck. And across the shoulders. Living on this island even for a day was hard work. Studying in these conditions, which were in all other respects perfect for study, was pretty much impossible, I thought. I had to struggle even for coffee. As I walked along the only street in the hamlet, largely deserted, I thought about leaving the island, and by thinking that realised the extent of my imprisonment there. I made for the jetty, all the goods now gone, just lobster cages and piles of netting and rope, blue, that looked knotted and tangled together even if it wasn't. The cage I kicked off the side had washed up in the silt below, the tide was still fairly low, but coming in. Two fishing trawlers lay in the slime, each having beached as the tide went out, ropes extending down to them from the jetty, covered with slime at the lower part. It took me some time to notice, as I stood, that neither trawler had a name. Two dinghies were moored a bit further down, floating now, again without names which I more or less expected, though dinghies are sometimes, actually quite often named, as well as boats, and trawlers, which are always named. I sat on a mooring point and watched them, one trawler tilted outward, the other tilted toward the jetty so that I could see inside it. There was nothing much inside. I returned along the jetty and along the street to the inn, or the front room, which I entered. There was nobody inside. The books were on the mantlepiece wedged like before between pickle jars. It was less cold but not much less cold than outside. My cottage was hardly less inviting but it was a good hour's walk away and so I continued to sit, waiting. I sat like that for several hours, or what felt like hours, having nothing to do but look every so often at the mantlepiece, the pickles, the books, and then out the window. I sat and turned the winged vertebra over in my hands and waited and looked and put it on my thumb and waited with it like that on my thumb and took it off again and turned it over again in my hands. Much later I could see the trawlers which had risen so that the tops of them appeared over the jetty. There was nobody about, not even outside. I noticed that each chimney along the terrace smoked with the exception of the inn. Having nothing to do—no bag, or book, or distraction—I spent the time thinking about when exactly I might return to the cottage, in a moment, or perhaps not quite yet, but soon, willing myself to stand up and leave and take the walk, which was only an hour's walk along the track. Alternatively I looked at the pickles. I placed the death manuscript on my lap again, with the exception of the first few pages that I had turned over and placed face down on the small table to the left. I'd left my drink in the study, the coffee I had warmed which was now cold. It had been reduced pretty much to the undrinkable residue at the bottom of the cup anyway, the bit that lines the teeth and coats the tongue if you forget to stop before the last bit runs over the lip. There was far too much in this stack of pages, I felt, to read, ever, given that I found most of it to be completely unreadable, although there were parts that were not so bad, the best of which resembled my own thought and was actually pretty decent. Looking up at his ear, and the son behind it, who was still asleep, head forward, I decided to inspect the last pages of the stack, assuming they were also the last pages before it was dropped and reassembled by someone other than the man before me, the dead man, since I am sure he would have gathered the pages back and stacked them neatly like the stacks I used to see him carry, unbound always, but well gathered. The last pages were in the right place after all. They were titled *Coda* and were intended to bring things to a close and round off his analysis. *This is just a book without a publisher*, he would say to me, and I would look away embarrassed. Finding a publisher is a bad game under the best circumstances, even for me. I have always hated the labour of finding a publisher, although I have never failed, unlike him. I have always succeeded in finding some publishing house or other to add its authenticating stamp to my work. Publishers have always made themselves hateful to me by their insistence that I first tell them what my book is worth to them, by setting things up so that I must sell myself to them when they should really be selling themselves to me, when they should be knocking on my door, and not me on theirs, asking me for the opportunity, and not me asking them. For him it was worse, he would never find a publisher and rightly so because every publisher he approached was well within their rights to reject him as any self-respecting publisher must reject work such as his. Still, the *Coda* was not all that bad, I thought, as I read the first line, *The book in hand may well be rejected as a work of unmitigated pessimism*, it began. That wasn't entirely bad as an opening line for a *Coda*, and if he told the publisher to begin reading his manuscript at that point, they might not put it down outright and relegate it to the so-called slush pile, a hateful name publishers use, this slush pile, a term of dismissal used to disregard almost everyone unknown to them. It is the single term that sums up all the arrogance and dismissiveness of publishers and editors in this industry, I think, although in his case it was an entirely appropriate term to use, I could actually think of no better term for the situation of his writing, since there was no better place for his work than a so-called slush pile as publishers call it. Surely, he continued, if education and sickness are indeed connected in the manner above described, there can be no hope left. If education and sickness are connected so that there is no education without an element of sickness, he wrote, there can be no way of saving education from the sickness it produces. If education is permanently sick, or somehow sick-inducing, or sick-connected, it cannot be redeemed, just as education cannot redeem us if education always carries with it a little sickness. Education cannot make us better by design due to its pact with sickness. To the extent that this book is at all read, he wrote, I suspect it will be understood or misunderstood in these basic terms as an argument that must be ignored, undermined, and dismissed because of what it disturbs. It will be observed that the book in hand lacks hope, or leaves its readers in a hopeless predicament, as if hopelessness were itself sufficient ground to reject a point of view. Few people, in my experience, he wrote, are able to tolerate a book that leaves them hopeless, let alone a relentlessly negative book. Books completely *devoid of light* are rarely published, or at least hardly read, although by *devoid of light* I really mean *nearly devoid of light*, he wrote, since there can be no such thing as a book that is completely devoid of light. There is no such thing as a book that gives its reader no hope at all. Every book has some kind of hope attached to it, if only the hope of reading it, or of having it read. At its most extreme, a book may be *near hopeless*, and may point to the *near hopelessness* off its readership. That is all that can be achieved by a book like this, he wrote, *near hopelessness*, although this near hopelessness seems to be good enough reason to render a book *near unreadable* and *near unpublishable*, he added. This all explains the inevitable response this book must receive, he wrote, referring to the wad of paper, the unpublished, completely unpublishable wad of paper on my lap. In its argument that education and sickness are fundamentally connected, this book is relentlessly pessimistic, they will say, he wrote, or more sympathetically, they will write, *This book is a victim of its pessimism*, as if its author too were a victim of that pessimism and the book itself a monument to the suffering author. All of which amounts to just another set of excuses for not reading *a near hopeless and a near unreadable book*, he wrote. To the extent my book will have any influence, he continued, it will be found guilty of promoting despair, of sanctioning gloom, and of doing so at precisely the wrong moment, our moment of global crisis, when the worst thing we can do, they say, is lose faith, worse still attack education, or even just doubt education, given that educated existence is now said to be so vulnerable if not on its last legs. If there is, today, as many suspect, some kind of crisis facing education and the existence of educated people, who feel beleaguered and find themselves facing, so they think, the combined and rising forces of unreason, untruth, and destruction—their own apocalypse—if education is now burdened as never before with saving humanity, or at least their humanism or human outlook from obliteration, surely hope and optimism are required, they go on, not cynicism and despair, or outright negativity, *least of all dark curiosity*, which is perhaps my position, he wrote, although my position will be called *nihilistic* by others, or one of abject nihilism, or something like that, he wrote, when almost everyone who uses the word nihilism does not understand the word, has no appreciation of its extent, and will not admit that if I am a nihilist then so are they, because my nihilism extends so far that it swallows them up, in that they, too, are nihilists of the worst sort, being *unwitting nihilists*. These unwitting nihilists will take the book in hand, this *near hopeless and near unreadable book*, and they will decide that it is too much, too negative, too dark, too dreary, without realising, of course, that it is not half as negative, dark, and dreary as I would like. This book falls

short in that respect, I think, he wrote, and remains a book of my own
dark curiosity. But even in that form, the form of a book that enter-
tains its own *dark curiosity*, this book will be rejected, he decided. The
educated bleed on and on about the necessity of hope and optimism
at the very point their existence is questioned, if not directly—*because
when I address them, they do not heed me*—but as their existence is
questioned materially, he wrote. The educated find themselves questioned materially all the time now, as the so-called civilizing influence of education appears to diminish, as vested power considers the
educated an irrelevance, no longer needing the educated to veil its
raw nature, its violence, behind the fine ideas, fine sentiments, and
fine thoughts of educated culture. Only education, they say, can make
us what we need to be, and reveal the truth of the world to us so that
we may act upon it together in harmony, or collaboration, or some
other word that does the job. Only education will allow human beings
to respect one another as human beings. Only education will save us
from our animal nature or from our artificial nature, whichever is the
target and the villain. Only education will keep us from destroying
one another and the world we live in. The educated go on and on in
this way, he wrote, sensing as they do but not quite realising the
approaching irrelevance of their educated culture, and their refine-
ments, which have served power for centuries, soothing its operations, bridling them to some extent, but facilitating, thereby, the
continued violence of rule and authority by working as its cover.
This need of education by power, he wrote, is today finally being
dispensed with. They are right to perceive their irrelevance, he
wrote, but wrong to understand that irrelevance as something to
only lament. To suggest as this book does that education cannot
perform this given function of redemption—as saviour, as redeeming
teacher—and that education cannot do so because it is not designed
for that purpose, is an argument considered by educated people to be
at best wrongheaded, if not reckless, and must be a position that
places its author absolutely, and without question, on the wrong side
of history, he wrote, sounding a little too grandiose I thought. To
claim that education cannot improve or redeem us *because it is not
designed to* will be rejected as the worst kind of reactionary nihilism,
in league despite itself with the darkest forces that educated people

combat. But this judgement against my book is a further symptom of the problem, he continued. It reflects the very point of view this book has attempted to disturb, the judgemental frame from which a book such as this one will be rejected on the grounds of its pessimism. Positioning itself against that point of view, knowing it will not be heard, this book is *conscious to the point of boredom* of the typical argument which claims that pessimism, like cynicism, is damaging and to be deplored because it saps energy and support from productive human endeavour, from the labour of rescue and reconstruction that might otherwise assist and improve our chances of living a harmonious, sustainable future on earth. Meanwhile, I think, and I say to them, he wrote, the damage is done. Their fight for education is a terminal form of virtue signalling a final display of pomp, a funereal performance for the sake of an audience *that is sick with itself* precisely because it remains wedded to the idea of optimism, to its own toxin, holding up for all to admire one of the very tools that has caused, or at least assisted, the perpetuation of its violence. Optimists disgust me, he wrote. They actually disgust me. Optimists block critical perception, they hinder realisation of horror, and prevent the full calamity of life under the yoke of civilization from appearing, offering in soft or determined tones a holy lie for which they are celebrated and applauded or just simply admired or worse than that *liked* for not yielding to gloom, for giving another reason to live, although what the optimist offers is the last reason to live, a promise of life that is a basic deception, that does not describe reality or acknowledge our existence in its full abjection, or at least its constraint, but offers up a version of reality, padded, stifled, coddled, so that there is nothing to live with but stuffed up air and the pretension of a kind offering, the gift of optimism. When facing destruction, the optimist always gets off too lightly. So-called optimism of the will is a damaging formula. I hate that line, he wrote, which ends with the phrase *optimism of the will*, as if *pessimism of the intellect* cannot be allowed to subsist on its own. Optimism of the will pits will against intellect, hinders its pessimism, and promotes its own impoverished understanding of the condition of our times. The problem with education in its best, in its most admired form, he went on, is its determined positivity. The best educators are basically optimists, he wrote, and for that they should be despised. Optimists aspire to be educators and give others a lesson in their optimism which is why the profession is an utterly hateful profession and an entirely deceiving profession. Education is connected with the mission of optimism and should be questioned for that reason. Educators should be doubted precisely because of their optimism if not driven out of work for declaring it. As a so-called positive force, education, which must include every commitment to educated culture and every commitment of educated people, functions as a damaging distraction if not enabler of the very conditions it laments and seems to combat. The best thing the educated might do, he continued, especially guardians of culture and study, by which he meant us at the university, I thought, is to draw, he continued, from their— by which he meant our—considerable resource, their access to knowledge, their catalogue of destruction, and use each testimony to the violence of civilized life to better effect, *to educate against education*, he wrote. I had no notion at all what he meant by that phrase, this idea that we might *educate against education*, nor, I suspect, did he. The guardians of culture, he went on, might approach every monument they revere, in art, in theatre, in thought, as a memorial to the violence that made it possible, and learn to better speak of that violence in order to cultivate a pessimism appropriate to its object. That pessimism is already in mass production, it surrounds us, he wrote, it is not for the educated to own, nor can they speak on its behalf. See the seas, see the land—pessimism everywhere. It exists, it is widespread, even though the distractions of materialism and the false consolations of humanist culture still keep it in check, to some extent. If the educated still wish to act responsibly, to signal their so-called virtue, to act as secular gods, they might at least attempt to attack the latter, humanist culture that sustains them, their adoptive domain, if not join in destroying the former, material culture, capitalist accumulation, their still-lucrative companion in world destruction. Doubting humanism is not enough, he went on, it must be attacked, or at least actively doubted. Critics of educated culture should not rest from prodding what they doubt, relentlessly, *remorselessly prodding it*, to the point of insanity. And I write the word *prod* advisedly, he wrote. This work of destruction, the one I recommend, cannot be of a sort that reproduces the forces of destruction, the machinery of war, but will take the form of a retreat, a vicious, treacherous retreat. That is what I envisage. The critic of educated culture must shrink from that culture and recoil and curl back from it. Here in what I envisage, he wrote, the materials of educated culture, its books, ideas, and works of art, have one last function left to them. They will serve to educate the work of withdrawal and contraction and might even be retained in the years that follow *as monuments to a three-thousand-year spree of educated destruction*. It finished there with that flourish. That was the end of the *Coda*. I placed the pages back in the bottom of his pile. I found his use of *emphasis* coercive. His commas, too, were coercive to the reader, although less so, since his comma placement was more often unfortunate than coercive, I thought. His use of emphasis gave his writing an insistent tone that I did not care for at all and that I recognised from his speech and the forceful desperation of his eyes. His arguments were often sound or sometimes they were okay, but his delivery was appalling. It lacked poise and composure. It lacked class, actually. Whenever he used emphasis, italics, underlining, and so on, I could see him pointing at me, waving his finger, holding my attention as if he would put my head in a vice. For some time I sat not reading and not particularly thinking all that much until the son made a sound in his throat that stirred him a little, not to wake, but so that he moved his head back, and I sat again not entirely sure of myself, with his head in that position, as if he were viewing me between eyelashes or sleeping oblivious. I looked to the mantlepiece which was made of marble, or some kind of imitation of marble, and that formed a lintel behind the head of his father, and thought about the wooden mantlepiece on the island, the pickles, and the books, and the wait in the inn, or the front room that functioned as the inn, a wait that was considerable, until finally I was no longer alone as they filtered in through the door. The fire was lit, and the same thing happened with the barrel and the pouring of drink and then eventually the stew brought into the room, which I ate, nobody stopped me, and I also drank. I was not sure, as I looked up, if the last time I looked the son had his head back or his head forward. He was asleep in either case. I should really sleep a bit too. The mind plays tricks. His sleep would be easier than mine not least because he had chosen the more comfortable chair. He was also the chief mourner, first among sufferers, a role he could relax into. At the inn I was on a stool for the stew eating, a position that was nearer the fire which was eventually lit, although I had been by the window for most of the time, having waited hours for the stew in the empty front room. By the window was a bench and a wall that I could lean against. It was whitewashed. I sat there, leaning back, looking at the one street of the small port town, which was really just a hamlet, a single line of houses, and a jetty. The tide was coming in and the two fishing trawlers had risen with it. They were small, perhaps only boats. This would make the use of the word *trawler* an exaggeration. The son was still asleep. It is possible there are whole periods of time that I do not remember and cannot account for. These would be those stretches of time I have no memory of forgetting. Is the son dreaming of his dead father, I think, or will his mind have gone somewhere deeper into itself, I mused. I have not yet allowed myself to rest, perhaps I should. There are things in that room that I cannot explain according to their events. Times I picked up the stack of pages from the floor although I did not put it there. The coffee stain on my trouser leg, I cannot account for that. Eddy's *Unity of Good*, on the carpet, I could not account for that either. I took it back on my way to the kitchen, more coffee, one-part hot water, two-parts cold coffee, or thereabouts. It was a passable drink. I returned to the front room, the death manuscript, the dead father, and the son, and looked in the stack of pages to see if he had written any of his argument about Eddy into his so-called book. There were indeed a number of pages about Eddy. Probably some of these pages were the basis of what he had told me two months ago in his study. I could see that his father was quite normal, just a bit gaunt, so that when he stood he swayed a little. I was more struck by how he puffed out his hollow cheeks. They billowed at points when he spoke. I was determined not to look at his face when he talked like that. Not his eyes especially. *Mrs Eddy presented herself,* he wrote, *as a distinctly maternal custodian of the Church she founded.* She used the maternal assumptions, the reactionary formulations of her age, to teach fortitude, and command obedience. Eddy was the suffering mother of nineteenth century literature in physical form. Her story was the first testimonial of thousands that would become *Fruitage* to the book. As she described her own battle against sickness, she taught the triumph of the spirit over circumstance. As mother to the Church, Eddy offered, and I quote, he wrote, *a living illustration of Christian faith.* She was referring to her mother as she wrote that, but really she described herself as she stood and gave her mother's funeral eulogy in 1849 and said those words about her mother being *a living illustration of Christian faith.* When Eddy said that of her mother at her mother's funeral, she was not thinking of her mother at all. When Eddy spoke of her mother, and said the words *a living illustration,* she had only herself in mind. Which is hardly unusual, he wrote, since we almost-always have ourselves in mind at a funeral. Eddy was her own *living illustration.* Eddy recalls in her memoir how she followed her mother in suffering, how she became an exemplary sufferer herself as she was forced to draw on her own resources in order to rescue herself from pain and oblivion. Eddy would in turn become the dearly beloved *absent* mother of the Mother Church she established. Between 1890 and her death in 1910, Eddy withdrew to her home and lived in relative seclusion, refusing to make any further public appearances or correspond with anyone outside her inner circle. This was her final, exemplary move, he wrote. Eddy became the absent spiritual mother all would long and pray for. Her absence was the logical, physical manifestation of her denial of material reality. It strengthened her authority and established her presence before she was finally and definitely absent by the so-called unreality of her death. She established in life the framework by which she might be admired once she was gone. She established the conditions for worship in absence that would continue, and that my family still observed decades later, he wrote. As adherents of the Church attempt to live up to Eddy's example as an exemplary sufferer, as my family, my parents, submitted to the Eddy healer and the Eddy teacher, we faced an intolerable burden. As followers of Mrs. Eddy's example we were encouraged to take upon ourselves the labour of the forever inferior teacher or student who works in her image. My mother had to be inferior to her example, even as it killed my father, he wrote, she had to remain in her great pain in the shadow of the first sufferer, as she suffered herself, since Eddy must be without peer. Eddy could not be approached in suffering even so many decades after she had taken her own suffering to the grave. When Eddy lived, she was careful to rid herself of all rivals. Eddy excommunicated a woman from the Church in 1890 who claimed immaculate conception. A woman like that would be a fitting rival and could not be tolerated. After Eddy, mothers should not give themselves too much credit. Actually mothers are to be treated with suspicion. Mothers may even become agents of sickness, as Eddy wrote. There is a passage in *Science and Health* in which Eddy describes just how damaging the mother can be. In later life a deformed man will come to realise, Eddy writes, that *a deformity produced prior to his birth* was the result of *the fright of his mother.* Congenital defects are, Eddy confirms, the mother's domain, they are her responsibility and her guilt. Those who suffer them must blame their mothers. Mothers who fear for themselves bring upon their own sicknesses and the sicknesses of their children. Fear will not afflict those who know that they have no reason to be fearful. The mother's fear is her responsibility, and she will do damage to her unborn child by way of it. As Eddy writes elsewhere, he wrote, fear is *the foundation of disease.* The burden of the mother, as an educator and spiritual leader within the family and within the Church, is a heavy one, he admitted. But Eddy was not out of step with her time. The notion that a mother's fright might produce birth defects was not Eddy's invention. It was a nineteenth-century commonplace, he wrote. So much pressure fell upon us, in particular my mother, and it did eventually break her. She willed my father's death, as did I to a lesser extent, as did my father will his own death, so the Church taught us. We willed it because when he became ill, we noticed his illness and by noticing it made a reality of it. We thought, he is dying, and he died. We willed it because our will had not been silenced. *Christian Science silences human will,* Mrs. Eddy taught us, but we did not silence ours. We knew, but we could not put into effect, her teaching that human will is *the cause of the disease rather than its cure.* As we willed the death of my father, we did not properly understand Mrs. Eddy's lesson, which declares, *the power of the human will should be exercised only in subordination to Truth,* where that Truth is revealed through study, and by the example of the Leader and founder of the Mother Church, our Leader, Mary Baker Eddy. I suspect, he wrote, that all this will look extremely odd to anyone who is not and has never been a member of the Church that brought me up for the first decade or so of my life.

These lines will be read as descriptions of something entirely alien to normal perception for most readers. Most readers will consider Eddy's religion to be, at worst, anti-modern, at best, atavistic. But Eddy is entirely modern, he wrote. She is a modern archetype. She teaches from a position of self-assured belief and domestic piety rather than medieval sinfulness and endless atonement. Eddy supersedes medieval perception by adding the portentous idea that suffering, as illness, is the exclusive doing of the individual sufferer. God no longer has any hand in it, she tells us. For the Christian Scientist, God does not punish or teach through sickness. There is no lesson in sickness, only error. In Eddy's modern religion, the sick individual is doubly charged with having *directly* produced, and then having to remedy, their disease, which was their error. This might sound intolerable, if not perverse, but it is familiar, he wrote. We just don't see the connection. I grew up taught to think that the Church my mother rejected was entirely perverse. My mother told me as she turned from the Church and when I was still a child to no longer blame myself, as she would no longer blame herself, and blame my father, for willing his death. She told me it was the Church that killed him. She told me this as she sat by my bed and as I readied to sleep. She said that she would destroy the Church if she had the strength. As she sat there by my pillow, she said that she would annihilate it for what it had done to us. That it was her duty, as my mother, to annihilate the Church which first brought me up. Only she did not use the word *annihilate* but used Eddy words and the Eddy idiom. It was clear to me, as I lay listening, that although she used Eddy words and the Eddy idiom, she had a minor genocide in mind, *a minor genocide*, I thought, or later thought, since to annihilate the Church must mean to obliterate its activities which are the work of the faithful, and not simply obliterate the work of those at the top of the organisation, its foremost deceivers. It would never do to target the foremost deceivers. More must be done than merely obliterate the Mother Church at Boston and all those of first rank within the organisation who might be gathered inside. Wiping out the Mother Church at Boston would obviously be a start, and flattening all those inside would help make a point, but it would not, for my mother, be enough to satisfy her demand that the Church which killed my father, and which killed others too on a regular basis, should be annihilated. People die all the time of preventable diseases, she told me, as I lay there tucked up for sleep. I think my mother wished to wipe the Church out of existence, completely, so that there was no residue of it left except her pain, perhaps, and the pain of others like her, those who experienced pain like my mother, knowing it to be real, those who were assured, finally, of the materiality of their suffering, no longer believing or trying to believe or taught to believe that their pain is an illusion. But then she lost her Eddy words and the Eddy idiom which were the last traces to leave us after the faith left us and the change of church brought other teachings to our home. We were so used to the Eddy lexicon that it was second nature to us to express our strongest thoughts in Eddy terms. Only long after we had left the Church did we find other words that came just as naturally as Eddy words once did. It took time to find other words that were not Eddy words, which felt just as authentic as they were expressed, and not forced as if we were using another's words to express our feelings. Gradually we became accustomed to the new church, which was ordinary, and did not pervade our everyday speech, and so the thought of annihilating The Church of Christ, Scientist receded, or at least she no longer mentioned it. She tucked me up in bed now without mentioning at all the idea of annihilating the Church, which is not to say that I no longer thought, as she tucked me in, of flattening people, for instance, under the Mother Church at Boston, and asked myself as I did what else might be needed to annihilate the Eddy influence. I thought about that a fair bit. I remained fixated on the religion she rejected, retrieving all the Eddy volumes she threw out and stowing them in my bedroom so that I might, when no one was looking, spend time with the forbidden books, and mull them over. My mother found them, and she binned them. I found them binned, pulled them back out, and so it went on until she no longer binned them but stowed them elsewhere in the house. Oddly, she never destroyed them. I checked the stove and the fireplace, but they were never there. With Eddy still part of my childhood, forming its backdrop, I was surrounded by Eddy words and Eddy ideas even though I could no longer mention them to my mother, or anyone else. They were censored, unreasonable thoughts, words fit for annihilation. But the world about me seemed to reflect the thoughts I had, the Eddy words I mulled over but had no place to express, or person to express them to. The Eddy books seemed not at all peculiar when placed in my mind alongside what I saw and experienced. I came to think that what I saw and experienced outside The Church of Christ, Scientist, was just as fit for annihilation as the Eddy influence my mother no longer talked about obliterating. I no longer merely thought of flattening people at Boston because the task had broadened well beyond that. When I placed the Eddy books alongside all that could be talked about and was taken as given in the world about me, their strangeness seemed less assured, or to put it differently, the world I saw seemed just as strange and just as deserving of annihilation. It mirrored the Eddy books that I read. Of course, he wrote, the world I saw did not mirror the Eddy books from the perspective of a believer but from that of a non-believer who sees the logic of the text but does not subscribe to it. The logic of Mrs. Eddy and the logic of the world were not always so far apart, I thought, he wrote, which is where my life's work began although I did not know it yet. My work started with the inadmissible thought, certainly before my mother, that the church which killed my father was not all that different from the time in which we lived. My mother would have resented me for thinking that, he wrote, for diluting the malice of the religion that killed her husband, that killed my father, by seeing the same malice, or something similar, elsewhere about me. But that is what I came to think. Christian Science was not a grotesque outgrowth, an aberration, a strange and appalling religion, but represented in its Eddy logic the extension of a logic of existence that was busy killing other fathers and mothers and sons and daughters in droves, or if it did not kill them, it diminished them, squeezed them, and convinced them that their diminished existence was entirely deserved and, worse still, that they did it, that they had done it to themselves. I came to see that the same logic of existence which diminished members of The Church of Christ, Scientist, convincing them as it did that they were the agents of their own pain, clearly diminished others too. The same logic of aggression was in operation outside the Church and reached far greater numbers than the Mother Church at Boston could ever hope for, he wrote. The Church of Christ, Scientist was, so I came to understand, a distinctly modern Church and presented only one, peculiar manifestation of the modern tendency to destruction which declares, as the world faces oblivion, that this great tendency to destruction is not all that lamentable as if it did not properly exist. It can lament the destruction it causes, assuredly, and will cause those who lament it to blame themselves individually, but it will only half-lament the destruction it wreaks, since to fully-lament that destruction would mean an end to the destroyers and their way of life. I always felt that a total lamentation was necessary, a total lamentation that would at the same time be a total destruction, and which was only the logical conclusion of everything I saw about me. The modern tendency to destruction is associated, he wrote, with an Eddy-like denial of its material effects. Since what does Mrs. Eddy teach, after all, but the unreality of a world that is bent on its own destruction. Or, more distinctly, the Eddy-like denial of a suffering world is tied to the relentless positivity of that denial, where, according to the outlook of that relentlessly positive disposition, the worst creatures on earth are, apparently, those who focus on the fact of destruction, who perseverate on destruction. Against that apparent sickness, against the sickening effects of negativity which even doctors hold to be true, the Eddy lesson presents optimism, the mind-cure, the mental oblivion of hopefulness, optimism as the route to salvation and Truth. Those who lose hope, who focus on the presence of disease and pain, who remain determined in their gloom, are the real destroyers of the world, or so the Eddy-lesson teaches. The world, as I have known it, he wrote, faces destruction with the same attitude, denying the full reality, the full horror of material existence, and so repeats all the same mistakes and habits that, as anyone who cares will know, are responsible for its obliteration. Optimism is its own route to apocalypse, he wrote. This all became apparent to me at school, he continued, where I encountered and had to live through years of petty malice, desperation, and cruelty, which was never properly talked about, we did not have the words or space to discuss it, and which was all of it justified, if only implicitly, by the optimism of enforced, relentless work and study, sore arses and straight backs, as if the single-minded stupidity of institutional life was the only route to adulthood. The local school I was sent to at eleven was, I came to think, the secular equivalent to the Church my mother abandoned and wished to annihilate. It carried the same double burden of the faithful, where Mrs. Eddy teaches that the sick and suffering Christian follower of the Mother Church is not only responsible for healing themselves but has caused their sickness in the first place. Those who taught me faced similar blackmail, and we suffered blackmail as their students, though we dealt with it better. We were able still to laugh at our suffering teachers, and make them suffer even more out of pure, youthful exuberance. Teachers are given sanction to educate, to enlighten, and alongside that to corral and abuse, but teachers fail in multiple respects to fulfil their mission, or its higher purposes at least, never failing to abuse, and most often succeeding to corral, but permanently failing to enlighten. The entire environment of the school declared, as we failed, that only we were responsible for our failure, that only we would be able to save ourselves by redoubled effort, and only we would pay the price of not heeding that lesson in later life, in poverty, or want, or from sheer dissatisfaction with our lot and what we had and had not made of our lives. As an adult I came to see this logic repeated at a more general, systemic level. The project of modern secular education is similarly burdened with the blame of having helped produce a dysfunctional, unreasonable society, and having then to remedy all social maladies by educational means. Education is blamed all the time for its failures, and then offered as its own solution. More education is the solution to each example of educational failure, he wrote. Here again was another sentence that struck me as familiar, as if lifted from my own writing, although I could not place it. Having Mrs. Eddy in my head as I grew up, he went on, helped me to see that the world beyond Eddy was just as grotesque. The world beyond our religion would have killed my father too had he outlived the Church that had us kill him before the world outside had the opportunity to do so. Outsiders judge Christian Science to be perfectly insane, but I find the same insanity everywhere about me and left completely unremarked. It is the most disturbing fact of my existence, he wrote, that so few people look around themselves with horror, as I already did at an early age, and do not see the calamity about them, everywhere, in the worst places but also in the best. For the Christian Scientist who believes as Mrs. Eddy writes that *disease has a mental, mortal origin*, the mind becomes the agent of change through its re-education. To overcome their alienation from God and their preoccupation with the illusion of matter, those wishing to be educated must approach the teachings of the Church with openness and humility. They must demonstrate their willingness to change false opinion and attitude and reorient the mind. Old understandings will be replaced, Mrs. Eddy teaches. Here again, he claimed, Eddy clearly positions her religion as *distinctly modern*. Old superstitions must be superseded, including the idea of a vengeful God. In one testimonial of religious healing from Eddy's *Science and Health*, the battle of old and new understanding is presented as *terror before revelation*, as a resurgence of pre-scientific Christian prejudice. The testimonial is entitled *After Twenty Year's Suffering* and recalls the testimonial author's conversion to The Church of Christ, Scientist, and how *ignorance and the prejudice of old education produced such fear that I hid the book*, by which she meant her Eddy book, *under the covers of the bed whenever the children came into the room, fearing that it was not of God and would injure them*. Her fear was the product of her superstition, and that, like the illusion of her suffering, had to be done away with. *As an educational opportunity*, he continued, now recalling his earlier medieval analysis, *the hour of death* retains some importance for Christian Science, but it figures very differently, since death is an illusion like sickness and the last hour is no longer, strictly speaking, the last hour. Consequently, education is now faced with no clearly defined border, a place where education, like the body, reaches its limit and expires. To the medieval mind death had absolute educational significance. It was the high point of educational possibility. For Eddy, death has very little educational significance. It is just another error to turn away from. With the denial of death there is no clear terminus or finish line that might encourage the student of God to pick up his or her pace and make one last desperate and defining attempt to study well, after which all study must cease. With the denial of death there is no exact point at which educational endeavour stops its incessant activity and is replaced by communion with God. The crossover here with the attitude of modern secular education is remarkable, he wrote. Eddy's disavowal of death entails the disappearance of a border between material life and afterlife, a border that would define a space exterior to education. A realm beyond education no longer exists for Eddy, just as it ceases to exist from the perspective of secular education. In each case there is nothing to travel beyond, since for Eddy the material world is an illusion, and for secular education, there is nowhere else to travel to. For this reason, he wrote, we arrive at a point in history where there is no place where education can be said to have no application. There is no realm where education ceases to have relevance, and where educational activity ceases to make sense. In this respect, Christian Science unwittingly reflects the modern perspective regarding the necessary ubiquity of education, its ability to find application everywhere. A single choice confronts us, then, in modernity, he wrote. *Education or nothing.* There is only education or nothing and no place between. It is a beguilingly simple alternative, this *education or nothing*, he went on. Education has achieved such ubiquity in the modern era and has done so in such a way that the problem of education is almost completely overlooked. This reflects, he wrote, the absolute triumph of education as an organising idea. My suggestion, my idea, actually my great intuition, he wrote, namely, that the problem of education is the most serious problem of our time, will be dismissed, he went on, because there are so many other problems that are more easily perceived. To argue that education, or what I call the great educational conceit, is at their root, is at the root of all problems, will again face dismissal. The modern insistence that education is at the root of all solutions will not brook the suggestion, my great intuition, that actually education is at the root of all problems. That easy disregard of the most intractable problem of our time, he continued, only demonstrates to my mind the success of education as an organising idea. Since education faces no border, it is not restrained by any limit. Death is now viewed opportunistically, and functions like any other apparent limit point, as a potential stimulus for deepening the purchase of what I like to call, he wrote, *the educational imperative.* Death is just another opportunity to stir that imperative. Any consideration of death will merely advance *the educational imperative*, he wrote. Death is just another reason to submit to education because there is nothing else. It may sound a little melodramatic, but from the perspective of educated sense, which is really a kind of nonsense, the best that can be achieved is to die educated, or even better to die with some legacy, or leave a memory that will continue to educate others. The educated are obsessed with their legacy, a memoir if they can manage that, a novel written at last on retirement, or a set of diaries, or a well-positioned tree with a plaque, or a plaque on a bench, or in most cases just a set of memories, a set of photographs, a trace of themselves, an artefact, an heirloom, the desk your great-grandfather sat at, some kind of enduring influence or at least the simple self-assurance that they will not be swiftly forgotten as soon as they are gone. All of that is no consolation, of course, which is why the drive to become educated, and to become a person of significance in that respect, must never cease to depress us. For Eddy, the illusion of death may be approached as an opportunity to realise its unreality, and thereby secure one of the most difficult lessons of Christian Science. This is her opportunism. The approach of—the illusion of—death is potentially educative, Mrs. Eddy teaches. Although death is unreal, to the extent that it is still perceived, death may function to demonstrate the limits of medicine. One illusion may, in effect, be played off against another, Eddy teaches, he wrote. The illusion of death can be deployed against the illusion of medicine, where even those who shun the teachings of Christian Science right until that last moment must still eventually give up on medicine as they breathe their last, and realise it is all over and that medicine has finally failed them. *Failing to recover health through adherence to physiology and hygiene,* Eddy writes, *the despairing invalid often drops them, and in his extremity and only as a last resort, turns to God.* What is the last prayer of an otherwise Godless person but the admission that medicine has failed them, Mrs. Eddy tells us, where even those who pray in their last moment of desperation, and have no knowledge of Eddy, confirm what she taught as they see the eventual futility of medical science manifested before them. This lesson has come too late, however. The lesson which appears at the point of—the illusion of—death is no substitute for a continuous educational practice in which the Mind realises its immortal potential. *The balance of power is conceded to be with matter by most of the medical systems,* Eddy writes, *but when Mind at last asserts its mastery over sin, disease, and death, then is man found to be harmonious and immortal.* To secular taste this faith in the power of Mind to heal itself above and beyond material intervention will appear deluded, if not vicious. It denies medicine to the sick, or alternatively, it makes the sick and dying experience failure as they resort to medical intervention, and guilt precisely because they have need of it, just as it made us sick, and guilty, as we gave our father morphine to ease his dying pain. But the logic of modern education may still be found here, he went on. Mrs. Eddy manifests only more obviously the absolute separation between education and sickness, where education can only be thought of as an agent of health, as an intrinsic good, as something that can be corrupted, precisely because it holds such promise still to heal us, to save us from ourselves and one another, and save the world from the worst excesses of human artifice. In the face of ecological collapse, for instance, it is impossible to doubt education in any fundamental sense, since surely educated perception is what sees the crisis, records it, and suggests a way forward, and surely only educated people will do what they need to do, will restrain themselves and rethink their activities, if the planet they have perceived, and the version of nature that they have idolised, is to be saved. Having lived so long with Eddy words and the Eddy idiom in my head, I can see, he wrote, how close this is to the Eddy logic I have just described, only I now know as I did not know before, he added, that none other will see it that way given they suffer the very commitment to education that I deplore. It is unconscionable to suggest that education might be in league with sickness. But this is why we must study Christian Science, he wrote, because it brings out their co-implication and renders explicit what modern education must deny. Eddy does so by making her own disavowal of sickness central to her doctrine, where the Christian Scientist must not see sickness in order to be freed of it. It is a perverse denial for course, he wrote, since Christian Science still retains sickness in view—prominently displayed in the *Fruitage*, for instance— even if each ailment can only appear in the form of its rejection, as a love of Mind against sickness, and as a determined, oblivious positivity before the twin spectres of death and suffering. In a similar, less obvious way, he wrote, modern education is borne of an engagement with sickness, and exists in relation to it. Education, like Christian Science, is riveted on sickness though it will not declare or admit its dependence. Education is haunted by sickness but would prefer to proceed as if it had nothing to do with the sickness it produces and depends upon. The insistent positivity of modern education is the product of this reaction against sickness. Modern, post-Enlightenment education is based on a sick dynamic, he wrote, and then proceeded to list its key features. *First*, modern education is constituted in the opening created by its own imagined elimination. Education is based on a threat of the feared consequences for the individual, for society, politics, the economy, if its institutions are not established and extended in their reach to cover the entire populace. Educated existence is based on a similar threat of the feared consequences for the individual, for society, politics, the economy, if the values of educated life are no longer observed and no longer function as the presumed basis of civilized existence. The feared end of education, the suggestion that we are living the end times when it comes to the existence of reasonable, tolerant, just, and humane attitudes that are felt to be everywhere suffering erasure, is used as a founding myth and functions as the first act of extortion. In our age, he wrote, the feared end of education functions as the first argument for the necessity of education. *Second*, education presents us with the obstinate but reassuring face of its finitude. That face is *obstinate*, because in secular society, there is nothing beyond education to which we might appeal for help, assistance, or meaning. Since there is no outside, no realm beyond education, modern education and modern educated existence must resource itself from itself. That face is *reassuring*, because if all problems are educational problems, they are only remedied by educational means. Some will object, raising the problem of religion. Surely the persistence of religion in modernity, they will say, or faith more broadly, demonstrates that education is not trapped by its finitude. But this perception, he wrote, the educational perception I describe, the modern educated disposition I attack, does not eliminate a place for religion, even as it holds that there is no educational outside, that we are trapped by our finite existence, that we are attached to a thing, education, that cannot ground itself in some other place that is beyond question. Individually, and in small groups, it is still possible to derive meaning from elsewhere, he wrote, and appeal to realms that lie beyond our reach, in the heavens, for instance, or in stories of fate and residues of myth. But collectively, as so-called civilized people, we cannot draw upon those resources, not as a larger group, he went on, we cannot base our existence again within religion, because that would risk a return to the savagery of faith from which modern consciousness still flees at such great cost to itself (and all in its path). Education presents itself in its finitude, then, as the great but impossible redeemer. *Third*, education constantly reminds us that its demands will remain unfulfilled, there is only so much that can be achieved, there is a limit to how much culture one person can absorb, how many books one might read, languages one might learn, and so on, and besides, no amount suffices. It is on this basis that the educated are hurled and hurl themselves into the world-destroying preoccupations of performativity, the armed, full form of the educational promise. The relentless drive to expand the domain of educated people, in extent and depth, a demand which can never be satisfied because there is no definitive endpoint, no last achievement, no achieved understanding, well *that*, he wrote, precisely *that*, he added, is what helps produce the hyperactive, world-destroying impulse of educated modernity. Not machines, not capital, not imperialism alone, but the underpinning valorisation of educated existence is to blame for everything that educated people lament, he continued. The educated affirm their existence as one that will never be satisfied with the extent of its achievements. They suffer an undiminished sense of the unquestionable necessity of educated life, their existence, and that is what makes them unable to stop as they destroy everything they fear destroying and obliterate everything they would prefer to save, he wrote. Here again there was a relentless, almost totalitarian tendency to his thought, I felt. A commitment to destroy by argument, as if he urged himself to exceed what even he believed in thought and fact. As educational institutions accelerate, he went on, their development must in part entail the obliteration of features once associated with healthy educational environments. These earlier educational forms—mythological constructions in part—remain as ghosts, as executed, aborted forms of education and educated sensibility that return to haunt education with the extent of its failure. This returns the third movement to the first, he claimed, where the armed, full form of the educational promise both presents the threat to education and provides the stimulus to redeem it. The university, the school, is armed against itself, and repeatedly demands salvation. Educational effort remains riveted on the task it faces and makes for itself, rather than the sickness which created it. Here the advice of the Christian Scientist and the educationalist are one. So much effort has been expended, he wrote, *but the need of mankind is very great*, as my grandmother wrote in 1946, *and it behoves each one of us to practice these teachings to the full and to prove the truth that has been revealed to us*. Education is that truth. Education must be pursued to its end without question. Some things are beyond doubt. Education is one of them. *Man, being God's spiritual idea, can never be touched by any suggestion of material excrescence*, she wrote, that is to say his grandmother, who was writing in the *Christian Science Sentinel*. He had retrieved many of her articles from the Christian Science Reading Room in the city-centre, and this one was his favourite. He particularly loved the phrase *material excrescence*, I remember him telling me about it, going on and on as he did, that he and I were exactly that. He was *material excrescence*, I was *material excrescence*, his last neighbour before he moved to the country was *material excrescence*, even though we had to deny it, of course, because we were also, so we believed, educated people. We had to deny the fact, he said, that each one of us was *material excrescence* because we were educated people or at least thought of ourselves as educated people. He loved the fact that his grandmother had already made his argument for him, so he claimed, by insisting that Man, or *the educated* as he heard that word, *can never be touched by any suggestion of material excrescence*. The same goes for education, he wrote, and with that the page was done. I had taken the time to read all this because the Eddy book I had retrieved from his study, *Unity of Good and Other Writings*, was even worse, but still not as bad as looking at the dead father in front of me. The son was still in his seat, asleep, although I wondered if at one point his chair had been empty. I had a definite memory of his chair being empty. I had the clearest picture in my mind of his chair being empty so that I could see the back of it, with nothing but his father to obstruct my vision. But I had not seen him get up or move about, and as far as I could remember, he had been like that, his head forward, or his head back, but always sitting, and always asleep, or in a state that looked like it might be sleep, although at times I did wonder if he was watching me between eyelashes that were nearly but not quite closed. Everything his father wrote about education applied to me, in his mind. The death manuscript on my map declared it still, and argued, as it did, that I was just as much a victim of false perception as everyone else, including him. He was also a victim of what he laid out for attack, or at least he had to be according to his argument. That is to say, he would remain a victim to the extent he wrote in a manner that an educated person such as myself might understand. It was clear enough to me, as it should have been clear to him, that he deceived himself by using words that other educated people would be able to decipher. He was a victim of the same deception, I thought. He had to be, I told myself again. And that fact of it, of him necessarily being the victim of the same deception, is what gave his argument its absurd twist and made it impossible to verify. There was no way to verify his argument. As soon as his argument made any kind of sense to an educated person, it could not have been heard. There is no way of arguing against education, not really. There is no way of properly doubting education in a way that educated people can understand, I thought. Every argument against education must necessarily be a self-defeating argument and end up either as an absurd argument—an argument that can be safely ignored—or as an argument that has been tamed by its audience, an argument that has been rendered largely anodyne because it has been made understandable. His position was destined to become an absurd position and his logic would eventually become an absurd logic. However much he made that argument in terms I might recognise, it would always defeat itself. Even if he made it in terms that might get published—though his work would never be published because no publisher would touch it and no peer would rate it—*his argument would always defeat itself.* Even if he managed to convince me, under duress, since I was stranded here with his manuscript at his wake, his argument would always finally become a self-defeating argument. But this is what protected him. I had to regard him as absurd and reject him, and that immunised him as far as he was concerned from any kind of attack. It was inevitable, I thought, that I rejected him. Even his failure was absolutely necessary. We recognised the fact of his failure each year he stood up at the annual conference and delivered a talk, from the floor, not the podium, that nobody wanted to hear. He could only fail as he offered his argument against education, and if he ever realised that and actively knew it to be a fact, he was not after all entirely wrong in his argument. Even those who stayed to listen to him speak, out of sick curiosity, or in my case a sort of paralysis, had to see that he was failing as he spoke, and as we listened. He had no way of escaping what he attempted to critique, no way of getting beyond education, except dying, of course, but if dying was nothing, and he was presently nowhere, this was hardly an escape, only an annulment. It was education or nothing, as he put it, and he was now nothing, or almost nothing, having no thoughts to speak of, or impulses, or sensations of any sort, being entirely dead on the table before me. But I give him too much credit. I give him more credit than he deserves. He is not yet nothing. After all that, he lingers on, I thought, because I am still doing all I can to avoid looking at him laid there, his ear staring at me. Yes, I was now sure I had seen the seat beyond him when that seat was empty, but I could not remember his son standing, or moving about, and this indicated that I had, at some point, or perhaps at more than one point lost consciousness, and so had managed after all to loll into a kind of sleep, even though my chair was decidedly less comfortable than his. The son was now in his chair again, the more comfortable chair, with his head back, and seemed to be in the exact same position I had last seen him in before I began remembering the empty chair and thinking about the chair without him in it. I looked at the position of his shoulders which seemed to be exactly as they were earlier. I could not see his legs, due to the table, or the lower half of him, the waist and stomach, the elbows, but I could see the upper half of his chest, and the shirt he wore seemed, so I thought, to have the exact same creases as before, as if he had managed to sit down in exactly the same manner, and moved about subsequently in exactly the same way, so that the selfsame creases formed on the son's shirt. I knew that I had not studied them, but this was how it felt. Considering the creases, and the likelihood of them falling in precisely the same spot, which I remembered, and was sure about remembering even though I had not studied them or made a particular note of them, which introduced some doubt, I was equally beginning to wonder if I had indeed seen his chair empty and without him in it, proof, if that were the case, that

I had dropped off at some point, although I could not remember drop-ping off, or waking, only sitting here with his father's manuscript, passing the time by reading bits of it, and wondering, as I began to now think, if indeed I would, after the wake, have the energy to compare this fifth iteration of his life's work with the other three in my possession, because I could not really stomach the idea of reading the passages I had already read this night again, and not only again in this version of the manuscript, but again in the other three, to the extent that they reproduced, as he claimed, the same argument, and did so pretty much word for word. Once read was more than enough, I thought, and only under duress, due to the presence of the body, and the ear, and the son who might wake, and to whom I had promised in a moment of needless compassion, or guilt, that I would stay up that night with him, and his father, until they came for his father in the morning and shoved him in the ground. *To understand the relationship between sickness and education*, he went on, we must locate sickness within education, a process that will reconceptualise education so that it appears in its exemplary sickness. This sickness could only be hinted at in the prologue of the book in hand, he wrote, referring to the stack of pages on my lap. That hint regarding meconium was delivered as a passing insight, he wrote, derived of meconium, distant now, separated by so many diversions, necessary digressions, lines of thought. The intervening pages were necessary, he assured me. So many pages had to be written and worked through in order to return to the question of meconium. To come at the problem directly, to declare education sick, will only be received as it must be received as a perverse statement. The word *sickness* is so evocative, he wrote, that the thought of *medically sick people* will immediately replace the idea of the *educationally sick* so that the latter expression will appear excessive, if not in bad taste. *Medically sick people* get in the way of my argument, he wrote. Whenever I make my argument, I think about how *medically sick people* and those who care for these *medically sick people* will get in the way of what I have to say. To speak or write of education sickness is to risk immediate misunderstanding if not out-right censure. To spend so much time pointing to the presence of education sickness when so many people are medically sick, as they always are, is surely reprehensible, he wrote, which is precisely what he did, I noted. He wrote these lines even though he knew they were reprehensible. Two months ago, I saw him in his study, and listened to him go on about Eddy, having just myself visited a colleague in hospital who was medically sick, who had an actual medical sickness, and suffered it urgently. As I went to see him in his study, and he went on and on about Eddy, and I sat and listened, I thought about my colleague in hospital who was truly sick, not only apparently so. His son feared for his father, but his father's sickness was not a medical sickness, it was a work-induced sickness for which there was no excuse given how unnecessary his work was, not simply at a time of crisis, but at any time. There was no need for him to kill himself, as he had, by over-thinking thoughts that were needless thoughts and that had no audience besides. I might be blamed for my part in his death, but I had no real agency in it. His death was inevitable. His life's work had condemned him. It was just a matter of timing. And if I had quickened it, had I not done so, had I not quickened it, something else might have got him anyway, although what I had done more likely was give him a reason to live by causing his endless repetition of words, phrases, sentences, and paragraphs over the last four years. There was no reason for him to write what he did, given its pointlessness. There was even less reason to do so at a time of global crisis, since the basis of his argument, the idea of *education sickness*, was surely a repellent argument, or at least an inappropriate argument to make at a time of global crisis. At a time of global crisis, I felt, it is important not to indulge pointless thought and pointless critique, as he did. There is no sense or justification for doubting things that should be left undoubted and should remain undoubtable. To do so lacked sensitivity, I thought. His arguments were actually insensitive arguments and not simply pointless arguments. His entire intellectual project was an act of gross insensitivity, I decided. He felt, by contrast, as he told me, that at a time of global crisis it is more important than ever to doubt the undoubtable and pursue thought in directions that would ordinarily strike others as repellent. I had no idea why he thought that. At a time like this it is important to leave the undoubtable alone, I countered, and pull together if not simplify things in the process. It is important, in a time of crisis, I said, to focus on essential problems and not multiply problems. In particular, I told him, it is important not to bother and probe the very ideas we need to sustain us. He replied by telling me that our era is one great crisis, so that what I was suggesting, what I was actually suggesting here, was a reason to not think at all, all that much about anything, and to do so, or not do so, for a very long stretch of time indeed. I replied that really I only meant the current global crisis and that his response was a typical example of his tendency to exaggerate and distort perfectly reasonable ideas, such as the one I had just presented. When it comes to the life of the mind, as in all other areas, in a time of crisis it is necessary to adopt a kind of war spirit, I said, which he called *war stupidity*, even though the real stupidity, I felt, was to produce pages and pages of typescript that set out to examine and doubt the undoubtable *at a time of global crisis*. But still he went on, and became even more fixated, I felt, on his argument about the inherent sickness of education. He knew that he was even less likely to be heard in the context of a global crisis, but still he went on, typing these notes, thinking these thoughts. Even in a time of relative calm, security, and population health, he wrote, education sickness will not be apprehended. It was of course necessary to approach the problem obliquely at first, he continued, since education sickness cannot be understood, properly speaking, from within educated sensibility, crisis or no crisis. A sick sensibility cannot truly perceive its own condition. For instance, he wrote, a sick sensibility will ask in response to the accusation of sickness, just what health looks like, and will want to know by which standard of health it is being judged so poorly against. In order to declare something sick, it will argue, it is essential to have an idea of health to compare by. But that kind of argument, which insists on grounding every claim to truth in some absolute conception of health, of justice, or whatever, is yet another symptom of the very education sickness I have identified. *That impossible demand*, he continued, is just another reason not to think beyond the usual constraints and prohibitions that are placed on thought. My discovery of meconium, he wrote, allowed me to make connections that were otherwise denied according to the constraints of conventional thinking. It was worth introducing meconium, he wrote, in the prologue of the book in hand, even though I knew I would be misunderstood at first. Meconium was my basic argument, but it would not make sense until later. *Meconium*, the shit of the new-born, was absolutely at the core of my argument, he wrote, but I could at first only mention it in passing. It expresses perfectly all the dimensions of my thought. They overlap in meconium. Meconium is the perfect representative of my basic intuition, he went on. It is at the root of my thought. It is my great revelation. When I first encountered meconium as my first son emerged, when I asked about it and what it signalled, and discovered how very nearly my son had died even though he subsequently lived, all of this from the midwife who had an obvious *leaning towards melodrama*, as he put it, I knew that I had met the perfect substance, or been told of the perfect substance, the basic stuff of my surroundings, the tar-like substrate of civilized life. Education is, simply put, the making of people that more or less function in what we call society, and meconium sits at the root of it. My life's work coalesced at that point, around the question of meconium. It started to coalesce as the midwife with an obvious *leaning towards melodrama* accosted me in the corridor and told me of my son, mentioning the meconium he arrived with, and which declared it would be a difficult birth, *a more than ordinarily risky birth*, as she put it. Meconium allowed me to finally understand the nature of education, he wrote, the nature of education as a system of person formation, a system of person formation that involves a type of intoxication, he added, a submission to the law of educating others that is also a drug, a thing that destroys and diminishes as it intoxicates. The origins of education can be found here, I thought, or came to think, he wrote. Actually, I think my realisation occurred some days after my son actually stopped producing meconium and began to shit what the world, his mother, subsequently gave him to shit. His meconium was all out and gone before I realised its significance. Meconium is a liminal substance. It presents the last traces of foetal life, a life of mute sensation sequestered within the amniotic sac, he wrote, and it recalls a profound silence, the silence of the gaping foetal mouth ingesting amniotic materials, a silence that is only broken as the child cries upon birth. But it gestures forward too, since meconium is the first product of the child to be transformed. The transformation of meconium long precedes the development of speech. It is a biological necessity, for sure, he wrote, and occurs in other animals that shit meconium too, but with humans, he wrote, as meconium is noticed, and dealt with, and written about, and before all else *named*, it functions as a clue to the origins of education, and as such it is without parallel. It is the significance of meconium rather than the biological fact of meconium that I am drawing attention to here, he said. Man-made meconium is really without parallel, he went on. Education originates in meconium shit, he continued, and it resembles an intoxicant, or more precisely, it *is* an intoxicant, a drug pitted against other drugs, a super drug to replace all drugs. But education is also concerned with the production of waste. So much waste comes by way of education, he went on. Education, he wrote, is driven toward the production of waste. It takes the fabric of life and tears it up and shits it out. I did not turn to Aristotle by accident, he wrote. Aristotle set my argument up perfectly by writing *the child voids excrement sometimes at once, sometimes a little later, but in all cases during the first day.* Aristotle perfectly anticipated me, he went on, when he noted how *this excrement is unduly copious in comparison with the size of the child.* I turned to Aristotle deliberately, he wrote. It was inevitable that I would turn to Aristotle. I am not suggesting that education begins with Aristotle, he continued, or that it must find its roots in the tradition of philosophy associated with Aristotle, which must include his teacher, Plato, and *his* teacher, Socrates, as if a faithful lineage could be written of their deception. I am merely pointing out here, in pointing to Aristotle pointing to meconium, where the Western tradition of education in its global spread might still look if it were to attempt, as I do, to disentangle itself from the great conceit of Western supremacy which is contained, just as surely, in every self-lament about the West as it is contained more obviously in the worst excesses of Western imperialism. It is necessary, he wrote, to travel back to the self-professed roots of that conceit and find the very base of it in the shit that Aristotle noted and remarked upon when he reported that meconium resembles poppy-juice. The link suggested by meconium, the first shit of the new-born, to opium, connects intoxication to education at its self-told starting point, at the birth of European philosophy and the birth of the educated, cosmopolitan child. Think of education in terms of that first stool, he wrote, as an activity which begins as the new-born emerges and then shits, the shit of which resembles raw opium, an intoxicant, a route to new experiences which must also sicken the addict and so deaden the addict to the world. To think of education in these terms is to formulate the desire for education as a product of its own delirium, a kind of stupefaction, a sense of want, because that feeling of inadequacy, of ignorance, of *aporia*, must drive the will to educate and the will to be educated. There is no other impulse strong enough to drive that will to educate and be educated, he wrote. Education depends on ignorance. It produces the initial perception of ignorance, the very concept of ignorance, in order to offer itself as the answer to the call it first makes. The desire for education is manufactured as education is itself formed, namely, as an addiction to itself. I turned the page over and placed it on the table to my left. The son was still asleep. I stood up slowly, my knees aching. He did not move. I made for the door, very slowly again, and bent slightly at the waist. It takes time for me to straighten after a long period sitting. And that is probably something to do with my age, although even as a young man I remember walking about awkwardly after a long time spent sitting, too much time working as I had to work in order to become who I needed to be. I told myself as a young man that it was a mark of distinction, and that I had the scholar's gait, though really what I had was the kind of posture anyone who spends large amounts of time sitting will get, whatever they are doing. My strange way of walking had nothing to do with scholarship and everything to do with sitting, I knew. Still, there is a kind of sitting I do which is more than ordinarily slumped, since I spend so much time reading, and it is not necessary, when reading, to be particularly upright. Whereas someone manning a desk or driving a vehicle must sit reasonably straight, with a book it is possible to function perfectly well at reading in a slumped position. It really was the scholar's gait, I felt. And then there was the fact that I felt my back curved to the left a little. I have never been able to verify if my spine does actually curve to the left and I have never asked anyone to take a look, but I have noticed asymmetries in other parts of my body, and so it seems entirely reasonable to suppose that my spine does indeed curve a little leftward. This, I have told myself, owes to my preference when sitting to sit on the edge of a chair—which I adopt to vary my posture when reading, because bits of me start to ache—that is, my preference to sit on the chair, at the edge, and on one of my feet, folded backward. It is always the right foot that I sit on, and the right hand that I hold the book with. I have tried the left foot, but it feels entirely wrong, so that when sitting I lean to the left to counter the effect of persistently sitting on my right foot, since it is necessary to lean in the direction of the foot you sit on in order to maintain balance. It is this leftward leaning that confirms in my mind the curvature of the spine, and how it came to be curved that way, although I have not had it verified to see whether or not the curve is visible, or if that curvature is just something I have thought about so much it feels true. There is no way of checking myself because if I look in the mirror, I curve my spine. To complicate things, I sometimes wonder if my spine curves in one direction and then back in the other. When I stood at the inn, on the island, after sitting in the window for so many hours not reading but watching the two boats rise at the jetty, I struggled more than usual due to the cold whitewashed wall that I had been leaning against which had chilled my spine, and the fact that I had very little option to sit differently on that little bench, and so shuffled between a narrow range of postures, just enough to prevent the onset of chronic sitting pain. I moved to a stool so that I might have some of the stew that appeared, eventually, at the end of the afternoon, once they started to fill the inn. The fire was now lit, and that warmed me too, but the prospect of standing, properly standing, rather than the awkward half-standing manoeuvre from window bench to stool that had not required any kind of straightening, was not a welcome one given how long now I had been sitting. The stew was finished, they did not stop me eating it, and I sat before the bowl thinking about how I must now, finally, get up and leave the inn, since it was late in the day and soon it would be getting dark. I did not fancy walking along the track back to the cottage in the dark, I had no light, and the island at night was entirely black. Even in the port which was really just a hamlet there was not a single light along the street. They only had one street to light but had not lit it. Each house along that street had windows, and surely these would emit some light, but the windows were so small and so recessed in the thick wall of each dwelling that I could not imagine much light came out of them. I did eventually leave the inn with that odd gait of mine, which was easy in some respects, since I knew, I was sure they would not notice it, they hardly acknowledged the stew I took, and the bowl I took to put it in. But I put it off, I put off standing until the last minute, calculating the point at which I would have just enough light to make it back to the cottage. The pain in my lower back, my scholar's gait, was considerable as I left the inn and made along the single street. The tide was in and the two unnamed boats had risen to the level of the jetty. At the wake I am developing the same scholar's gait, again just as severely, I thought. The chair is padded and hence more comfortable than the window bench and the cold whitewashed wall, but still, it is the less comfortable chair in the front room, the son has the better one, and all things considered, given how many more hours I would sit here, I will be in a worse condition, or a condition at least as bad as the one I just recalled, which was extremely painful, so that I was still not halfway back to the cottage and the pain in my lower back, the curved part of it, had not yet properly subsided. I think I was only straightened, or as straight as I get, when I arrived at the cottage, since I recall raising myself to full height as I emerged from the hollow and as I walked past the bent trees, looking at the bad form of each with a kind of derision, thinking to myself how, in the morning, I really should hack off a limb and burn it. So it was entirely reasonable that at this wake I would stand, occasionally, and move about, though we were both holding vigil, and I should really keep the body company, or the son, I thought, and not leave the room to make coffee, or even just heat it up, and certainly not go to the dead man's study and start reading his books. I had made it to the door, but the son stirred a little, so I returned to my chair and raised the death manuscript again to my lap. Facing the ear, I decided again to read. We should begin by identifying the stupefying effects of education in its most easily denounced institution, he went on. That institution, of course, is the mass or popular school that emerges in the nineteenth century. It is no mere coincidence that the intoxicating effects of mass education took hold, he wrote, and became a matter of numbing routine, just as drugs were themselves undergoing mass production, mass export, and mass consumption, in particular opiates, which were mostly available without restriction or all that much control on their purchase and use. We should not be surprised, he repeated, to find that the dawn of mass education coincides, roughly, with the mass consumption of opiates, and then grows as the latter declines. The late nineteenth century pro-duced the figure of the addict and produced the modern school child. Each might be viewed as a response—circular, futile—to industrial society, he wrote. This was an interesting hypothesis, I thought, the idea that modern schooling, and mass drug consumption, originated in the same moment, and so shared characteristics, as he seemed to be claiming here. As the medical profession struggled to come to terms with addiction, he went on, and by struggling to come to terms with it defined it as a phenomenon, the entire pantheon of addictive behaviour was explained away as a *disease of the will*. The addict had been seduced, they felt, and, seeking relief from industrial society, took the easy route of delirium and drugged up euphoria. The will is addled, it is diseased and diminished before itself as the addictive habit takes hold, they thought, he wrote. Initially it was felt that the gentleman could take his opium like he could take his spirits, in moderation and with restraint, never losing control of the extent of his consumption. The lesser man and the weaker sex, the laggard, reprobate, and degen-erate, had neither powers of moderation nor those of self-control. Following each drug intake, the will of such types suffers a compul-sion it cannot resist as they seek ever greater oblivion and experience euphoria and bliss against returns of depression and desperation. The drug generates the condition it was taken to combat, or worse still, produces a cycle of abject compulsion that is even more dire than the condition it was first taken against. This addictive cycle, a downward spiral, was gradually understood, with the late admission that not even gentlemen could drug themselves without adversity. The con-nection with education may not be obvious, he wrote, but education came to function at precisely the same moment in like terms. The basic plot of education is the path of addiction, he continued, it traces a similar line from initial seduction, first happiness, and glee, to despair, abjection, seduction, repeated relief, worse symptoms, greater abjection, all of the above repeated, temporary recovery, eventual decline, wastage, and finally, death. The late nineteenth century drug user and the education advocate present a circular, destructive logic, he wrote. Both offered respite from the trauma or pain of existence in modern society, or, if not respite from trauma, simply release from the boredom of civilized life. Both answered the need and created the desire to seek experiences that everyday life does not provide, as greater numbers of citizens turned to books just as they turned to the apothecary for relief and distraction. These books were not always read, of course, which is the fate of most books. This was an addiction, in part, to the *thought* of reading them, and to looking at them, to feeling pleased at the purchase of them, taking pleasure at the smell of them, and the sight of others seeing them in one's grasp. As they submitted themselves to the multiple idiocies of book handling and book savouring, they established the basis of a habit, he wrote, and I read, some of which made sense to me, or at least I recognised the strange link between the love of books, or what he might call *the education sickness*, and the apparent need to self-medicate with books, to abandon oneself to them and even seek oblivion within them. I had observed precisely that during the most recent crisis, where at the onset of that crisis several colleagues told me how much they looked forward to a little time in seclusion with their books. They spoke of their regret at leaving the libraries empty, of how the books would have to talk to themselves, as they put it, but how at home they had so many books of their own, books they had bought with such good intentions and had never managed to read, and now they realised just how fortunate they were to have such a great unread cultural resource stowed and ready. Luckily, one told me, my house is overflowing with books, unread books, as well as those that have been read and beg to be read again. All of this carries me on, my colleague continued, and gives me a place to go and resource myself during this latest crisis and serves as a distraction from the most recent draconian measures the government has planned. As the restrictions began to bite, they sat at home, I thought, looking at these books, still thinking to themselves, so I imagined, how lucky they were to have amassed so many books, gathered over the years from so many good intentions in repeated fits of enthusiasm which took hold each time a book was bought but was shelved unread, the overall gathering of which was now finally paying off as they sat virtually immobile, for hours at a time, with all these unread books waiting for their attention. I did wonder just how many of their unread books would be read, and if my colleagues would indeed find the time or energy to read at home as they assured me they would, since there are so many reasons these days not to open a book. There are too many good reasons not to read, just as there are so many reasons not to write, life conspires against it, and so the books would remain unread for the most part but would probably even then be considered dreamily as a great fortune to have amassed for a time such as this. Once things improved and they came back, I did not ask, though I fancied asking, just how many of those books had been read, what solace they provided, and if they were still grateful to have such a wonderful cultural resource at home, if it made up for all the time they had spent sitting immobile, growing stiff, waiting to return. I was intrigued to know, although I did not ask, just what kind of solace their books offered and if they only picked the lighter ones which were easier to lift. So I had some sympathy with what he had written then, on this point at least, and some respect for the fact that he had written it before the crisis, though I found his greater argument about addiction a little hard to understand, or if not hard to understand, at least hard to agree with in terms of its scope and reach, given his tendency to over-reach himself so that even thoughts that had some potential were quickly destroyed by overdoing them. As I heard a marketing expert once say, a bad product is destroyed by over-marketing, by selling it too hard. He likewise had a tendency to oversell his ideas and so create a horrible disjuncture between the grandiose pretence he cultivated and the actual nature of his argument which was flawed and ill-worked through. *Each is a potentially fatal substance*, he wrote, both education *and* opiates, he confirmed. The addict lives in a collapsed realm, unable to recall how to organise their desire in the absence of the habit. The organisation of desire that preceded the addictive behaviour might be remembered, the life before addiction recalled, but the transition from one state of desire to another cannot be understood. It makes no sense to the addict how one became the other. The precise origin of addiction, he wrote, of the moment that willed behaviour became unwilled habit, remains inaccessible. With education, he continued, the time before the great educational addiction took hold remains indistinct. It is never clear where addiction began its relentless, devotional cycle, never clear what exactly was the point of health before addiction took hold, how desire looked in a state of health before observance became habit. At what point was educational activity *healthy*, he wrote, where *was* the threshold, who *was* the last healthy educated person, the enlightened philosophe of the eighteenth century, he asked, somewhat rhetorically, the first Renaissance humanist, he continued, or King Alfred the Great, perhaps, or was it before Alfred, the pious early Christian Monk, the philosopher emperor, the noble Greek. My knees were again aching. As I recall it, on the second day that I spent on the island, the second full day not counting the first half-day following my arrival, I woke again with my toes cold, my hands cold too, and my shoulders and my upper back with the cold air seeping in at the neckline. On that second full day, or the third day since kicking the lobster cage from the jetty, the looks I received, the inn, the *Take him to the cottage*, and the long walk, well on that second day I got up, so I remember, and did pretty much the same as on the first full day. With small variations, naturally. I lamented the hook and its absurd placement as soon as I woke, knowing that it would be a long boil. I think I didn't get out of my bed, which was really a cot, for some time, staring at the hook which I could see quite easily given that everything was in the same room. The distance from the bed to anything else inside that hovel was not far at all. The hook placement was obvious to me now and could be easily seen and lamented from the cot given that there was nothing between the bed and anything else in that room, with all the furniture, including the cot, set against the squalid walls. There was absolutely nothing to block my view of anything else. The hook in particular. I had first thought of the walls as rustic, but now, having stared at the wall closest to my bed quite a bit, considered them squalid. The walls were absolutely squalid. I sat up, if I remember rightly, and did so with difficulty considering how cold I was, and started to move about that single room between the furniture pushed against the walls, the table by the window, the cot by its wall, and the stove that I could not quite figure out how to work which was built into another. The trip to the woodshed. The fire, building it, blowing it, abusing it and myself for it going out. Eventually the fire took, and I hung the kettle for the slow boil. I sat with the coffee and the bread and cheese looking through the windowpanes to the trees. The three manuscripts, second, third, and fourth iterations there on the table, and I did seriously consider opening them, but went out, initially for a short walk, but soon enough for a longer walk past the trees, into and out of the hollow, over the rise, and down through the rift in the cliff to the shore, the tide out, where I took off in the direction of the hamlet. The skull was still there. I placed it on a rock and continued. I passed the other vertebra and placed it on a rock, holding the winged one still in my pocket, and made from one headland to another until I reached the larger recessed bay with the frogs. It occurred to me that I might have brought a pot to transport them in, perhaps the kettle once cooled would have done the job. I might have cooled it whilst walking, even, rather than wait for it to cool before leaving the cottage. But the froglet at the base of the cliff was gone. There was only one froglet left in the pool higher up, which I looked at and which looked back at me in silence, I thought, though really I could not tell if it looked at me at all, it was so small, the eyes were only where I imagined them to be and it did not move or flinch at my sudden appearance. When I passed the mine in the cliff, I did not go in but considered it, sitting for a while on a boulder below the rope that hung from the entrance. When I stood up, I placed a small stone where I had been sitting, for no particular reason, and continued on to the hamlet. I waited as before for the stew, and once I had eaten that, made off for the cottage before dark. On the third full day I got up pretty much as I had done on the second day. I took the kettle this time to the bay with the frog but the frog was gone, and so I found myself sitting in the inn next to the kettle I had brought, staring at the kettle, and staring out of the window at the two boats rising by the jetty until the stew arrived, after which I took the kettle back with me so that I might hang it for coffee the next morning. On the fourth full day I did again pretty much the same, walking this time without the kettle. On that day so I remember there were two frogs. I could not account for them and had no kettle. The skull was gone. On the fifth I am not sure if I brought the kettle or not. On the sixth I think I did bring the kettle, considered again hacking off a limb but forgot all about that as soon as I left the cottage. The mud was dismal. It had rained so that the muck in the yard was far harder to cross without wetting my feet. The shoes I had were falling apart from all the walking. The hollow beyond the trees was also pooled and the track almost submerged by the spread water. I am not sure why I ventured out that day. There were no frogs. The skull was back but further down. On the seventh day I readied for the ferry, packed the manuscripts, and made off via the cliff, the shore, the headlands and so on, because of my curiosity about the frogs. Again there were none. The skull was gone. The stone was still on the rock below the mine. I did not wait in the inn but on the jetty. The ferry arrived and I departed. I did notice that the lobster cage was no longer washed up and the two boats were also gone. I returned a week earlier than planned since I had hoped to be away for a good fortnight. He was as I feared still looking for the manuscript and came to visit me more than once. I am not sure if he suspected me although he did look at me oddly, and perhaps he was right, and I did look odd. Within a week he was working again on the great rewrite and did not bother me any further. The fifth iteration, the death manuscript on my lap, must have been horrible to write, worse than the fourth which would have been worse than the third and the second. I was reminded again of the superstition that my grandmother on my mother's side had me listen about in the garden concerning her death, where on the point of death, she said, the mind travels further than it should within a fragment of time and covers a vast space, filling that last second with an impossible quantity of thought. She believed, so she told me, that when she died this last second of her life would last an age, and that a whole series of thoughts she had never lived would occur to her, ideas she had not yet had would appear, and memories would take form that referred to no pre-existing history alongside those that did but that she would experience in their full magnitude, all of which she would be unable to communicate because there is nothing to say in that last moment, beyond exhaling. I was very young when she told me this, so perhaps it was just a story to spook me with. But it was also a confession of sorts, I thought, a deliberate confession perhaps intended to counter the religion that had taken hold of my family from my father's side, the religion that taught us death was nothing, that it was unreal, and so on and etcetera. Here, I thought, or later came to think, my grandmother played off one superstition against another. She countered my superstitious upbringing in The Church of Christ, Scientist, with her death story, her extraordinary superstition. Time expands, she said, and fills with so many things that have happened and been thought, and so much that has not happened and not been thought, none of which can ever be communicated because there is no time left to do so. As it turned out she died under a tram. She was taken along by the front of it some way, and was entirely dead, I like to think, by the time it stopped, lodged half under and half out, sticking out like that by the kerb. I saw it happen because she had just left me to cross the tracks. I watched the tram collide with her, take her with it, and eventually come to a halt with my grandmother half and half like that, the half bit that was sticking out stuck up at an odd angle. I stood and watched her taken along and under before I had the chance to think all that much about what it was doing, and what had happened moments after my grandmother said goodbye. The tram halted, the doors remained shut, and there she was sticking out at her angle. She was some way up the track because of how she had been pushed and the distance it took for the tram to come to a halt. Trams drop sand to help with the brakes, so I gather. I like to think she was killed instantly before she was taken along or very nearly instantly at least. I was not told which it was, if I asked, and I am not sure that I did. At the time, not knowing what to do, I walked directly home. I saw her sticking out, and turned, and walked home. I went upstairs and sat in my room and said nothing. I went up as I recall and sat there until they came and knocked at the front door and brought the news to my parents of the unreality of her death. Her superstition was a fine superstition, I think. It was a consoling idea to pass on as I have often thought, a nice idea to think with even if it only seems applicable to a bed death and not a tram death, but as an idea, and about this I was sure, it hardly applied to him on the table before me, since if he had an epoch to think and imagine, surely he would just repeat himself. He was by now so habituated to repeating his argument that I could not imagine if what my grandmother believed was true, which it wasn't, he would have the capacity to fill that vast realm of thought with anything remotely new. But that was an absurd thought, I told myself, looking at the son and not the ear, opening the manuscript again to distract me from other more disturbing thoughts that began to flash before me of his ear and how it listened at me, and then the thought of its cartilage, just the word cartilage is enough to get me feeling sick, the word has always disgusted me, and other strange notions, some of them formless, that happen when the mind is exhausted and in desperation produces utter rubbish. I could tell that my mind was beginning to produce that nonsense, or that it had already begun to produce nonsense. First, I saw my daughter. Then I had the sensation that the room was filling with water, and that I could feel it in my socks. And after that I thought I saw spiders picking towards me down the walls and across the floors from the periphery of my vision. The nonsense of sleeplessness, I thought. Someone I was once very fond of called this her spider sense, it was her spider sense, she said, that came upon her when she was particularly tired, or stressed. She could feel them crawling towards her, crawling up her, creeping in her hair, even though they were not and she knew they were not and this was only her spider sense as she called it, something that affected her, as it struck me too, when we were particularly fatigued. Clearly this was nothing but the nonsense of my tiredness. When I saw him sitting and no longer lying on the table, I knew this was the usual nonsense, my ordinary nonsense, and nothing special. I turned deliberately for focus and distraction to the manuscript, not to find out more about his thought on addiction and on opium, which I cared nothing for, or his thought on education and so on which I cared for even less. His manuscript helped distract me from the ear, the body, the presence of death and my sleeplessness, even if the manuscript dwelled upon death at points and was itself macabre. Struggling against the nonsense and odd notions and swamp-like feelings that penetrated my reading too, I came to read about Friedrich Engels and how Engels saw the connection between opium and education just as he on the table saw that connection, although he saw the connection better than Engels did, of course, as he claimed. Engels. I read. Engels. I kept on reading the name Engels. That name. Engels. I read the name Engels to focus my mind until the nonsense and the swamp-like feeling started to retreat and then was gone. Engels, I read again. This Engels, he wrote, saw an obvious connection between opium and education. He mentions it in *The Condition of the Working Class in England.* In that book Engels writes that education is precisely the solution needed to the *custom of giving children spirits, and even opium.* How can the poor be blamed for doping their children, Engels writes, *how could they obtain a more suitable regimen so long as they cannot adopt a different way of living and are not better educated*, Engels asks. Opium must be replaced by education, he wrote. Engels, like Marx, was just another stooge of the education sickness. For Engels, just as for Marx, just as for anyone else, *education follows opium*, that is their presumption, although Engels realised that education is not simply an alternative, *but a substitute*, for opium. At least Engels realised that, he wrote, at least Engels was honest enough to recommend education *as a substitute* for opium. Education is the great addiction now, he went on, and anyone who refuses to admit that clearly has something wrong with them, he wrote, as everyone does, he added. Schooled children became the healthy alternative to drugged-up children at home, just as the schooled child was presented as the healthy alternative to child labour. *Every last one of us must become intoxicated by education*, he wrote, *or incarcerated*, he added, perhaps both. I looked across the body. The son was still in position, his head forward as if he was not actually asleep but intently looking at me. I could not see his eyes in the shadows of his brow. He was looking through his brow like his father once looked at him. Him and the ear. He looked like someone I knew. It was unsettling to look at the son and think, *You look like somebody else.* I find it difficult to remember faces, perhaps everyone does, even those I know well I cannot recall so that I have to look at them to remind myself what they look like. I have a vague idea, of course, but not a picture or anything like that. Just an impression of a face I know so well but cannot form in my mind. With my daughter it is different, I can see her face clearly. Children are still found to this day, he wrote, whose apparent flaw at the last assessment is their failure to find education sufficiently intoxicating. These children will not be intoxicated by what education has to offer them. The drug is administered but it produces sickness without intoxication. The child sits, apparently inert, seemingly untouched by education, and *that*, he wrote, is the only education-related sickness that education can see. I had by now endured enough of his opium lesson. Education inherits all the complexity of opium, he wrote. Education inherits all the complexity of opium just as education inherits the complexity of religion. My argument must not be misunderstood on this point, he continued. I write at the risk of a great misunderstanding, he went on. I must write against that misunderstanding, he underlined, even though it is inevitable that I will be misunderstood because no educated person will ever fully appreciate the meaning of my words. To suggest that education came to function as a substitute for opium, he continued, should not be understood to imply that education replaced opium as a soporific that would pacify the masses. It would be a mistake of the first order to think that education replaced opium purely as a soporific, he confirmed. This would be a very basic and a very narrow reading of the replacement of opium by education, as if all education did was to deaden the masses and place the working poor in a state of contented, placid stupor. This would be a gross misreading, he went on, and a gross misdiagnosis, he added, and it is certainly not what I have in mind. If the great educational project of modernity inherits the complexity of opium in all the senses that I have come to know it, he wrote, education does not dull the population into submission at all, rather it *stimulates* the population to think strange things, to think perverse thoughts that accommodate the population to its own sickness. What, after all, are the thoughts of a sick population but perverse thoughts that accommodate the population to its own sickness, he wrote. The thoughts of a sick population can only be perverse thoughts. A sick population can only think perverse thoughts. Think of everything that opiates did, all they were employed for, he went on, and apply that to education. From the opium elite to the treatment of dysentery, he wrote, right through to Marx and his carbuncles. Education, like opium, stimulates the population, it *constipates* it, it cons and misleads it, it serves as its pain relief and soothes its boils. He was, I could see, really gearing himself up in this text, on my lap. The son still lay, head forward. Inert. I thought that by now I really should be feeling pressure in my bladder from the coffee. It was odd, I thought, that I still felt no pressure in my bladder. Resolutely circular, he went on, education functions as a propulsion system that populates its own fears, first among which is the notion that there is nothing outside education and educated sensibility but unmitigated disaster. Opium, like religion, once promised great things—heights of intoxication, pain relief, conquest, and health—but delivered great suffering. This inheritance was carried forward in the opening years of the twentieth century, he went on, as the education-addict exceeded the figure of the drug addict hooked on opium, ether, chloroform, or whatever. In this shift from great intoxication, or crapulence, to education, he wrote, the sober, aspiring, working-class man with a taste for self-improvement appears. This is the point, he repeated, that the working-class man with a taste for self-improvement takes the stage and begins, like the rest, to think perverse thoughts. This is the poor man bent on self-education, he wrote, the man who is admired for his commitment, the man of humble beginnings who turns to books, self-help, evening improvement classes, and museums of wonder and cultural enrichment—a perverse environment for perverse ideas— and finds that all he can think are perverse thoughts. You cannot blame a man for spending his last pennies on a bag of chips, for desiring just a little warmth, a moment's satisfaction, it has been said, but you can blame him for failing to improve himself, for failing to educate himself and failing to educate his children, he wrote, *for failing to pervert his children*, he added. As with opium, so too with schooling. If children were not yet sick enough for it, it would make them so. For a period, the two shared the same institutional space. Opiates were used in foundling asylums, as a sleeping draft from which many children did not wake up. It kept the orphans quiet and killed a good few in the process. Opiates were still in use at the beginning of the twentieth century, even though they had become largely unnecessary with the development of teaching and school architectures designed to maintain the masses in their submission. In the first decades of the twentieth century, he went on, opium was finally outlawed and replaced by a more sympathetic and enlightened treatment of the young, a treatment that was also a mistreatment, of course, he wrote, a treatment that was also a maltreatment, an utterly sick-making enterprise that took hold as mass education produced a sickness, the sickness it produced became a demand, and the demand it made was answered with a remedy. The remedy, being itself educational, would generate its own addiction, where the addiction to education demands more of the same, feeding the sickness that produced it and requiring higher dosage at higher levels. This addiction and its sickness were already well-developed in the elite classes. It was their gift to insist that all must wish to have their children educated, at some basic level, so that they may travel where their guardians fell short into state-sanctioned idiocy. It was a gift of well-disguised malice, he wrote, and I wondered again when exactly the coffee would make its way through me. I thought of the frogs. On the fifth day I probably did take the kettle to collect them, the fire long gone out by that point as I arrived in the more recessed bay, the one with the lower cliff, and looked at the slime where they sat or once sat, although it was not entirely clear to me when they sat and when they did not sit. I could not understand, sitting there, how exactly the coffee had not yet made itself felt. It was a mystery to me how the coffee had not made its way to my bladder. No, we do not serve coffee, she said, you must not drink coffee, coffee will do you no good. The son still sat. His chair, I felt, had been empty, but I could not remember seeing it empty, just the feeling that he had left the room. My own chair felt less bad than earlier, a sheet over my knees keeping them warm although they still ached below it. It happens that my knees ache when I keep them bent, or straight, for any stretch of time. If only I could bend them. As it became light or not so dim, daybreak less obvious due to the heavy curtains, or blinds, or the fact that there was no window on this side of the building, I looked up again at the son who was now clearly awake and looking back at me. It was a familiar gaze, I realised, now I could see the son in the light. That face is the reason why I stayed so long. Most probably the only reason I was still here, the reason I agreed, that I decided to stay, is that when I first saw the son last evening as he opened the door, he looked somehow so much like my own daughter, that I was for a moment confused. She had left me at the gate. She stood there, at my bedside, holding Bernhard's *Extinction* as I walked down the path and met the son. She put *Extinction* in my hands, and placed her hand upon them, and looked at me with that look she had, and then passed me my papers, and a pen, and held my hands with that look she had as I walked down the path to meet the son. I was more biddable than usual before the son who looked so much like my daughter and so I was susceptible to the words he spoke, as he passed me the papers, looking so much like my daughter, saying, *You must make something of these*, and added as I recall, *Do not leave me behind with them*, *Do not go*, *Stay and finish them*, she said, after which I held them and rested back, my hand in hers, and thought, what she really wants to do, in this room, is to keep me here. Her invitation to think, to write, is merely a pretext, all of which reminded me of my grandmother's superstition which I have always considered a pure but consoling delusion.

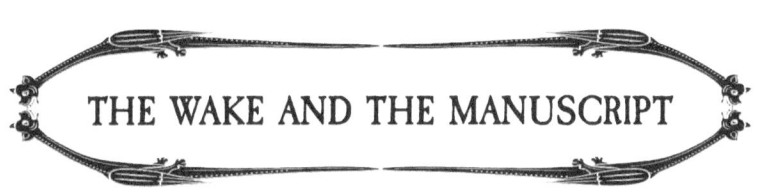

THE WAKE AND THE MANUSCRIPT

ANSGAR ALLEN is the author of the short history *Cynicism* for MIT Press's Essential Knowledge series as well as the novels *Plague Theatre*, *Wretch*, and *The Sick List*. He is editor-in-chief of Erratum Press, and he co-founded Risking Education, an imprint of Punctum Books. His writing has been published in a range of journals, books, and media, and it has been translated into Spanish, German, Estonian, Japanese, Mandarin, and Greek. Allen lives in Sheffield, England.

ANSGARALLEN.COM
ERRATUMPRESS.COM

www.ingramcontent.com/pod-product-compliance
Lightning Source LLC
Chambersburg PA
CBHW020653260626
47157CB00008B/3015